the Waiting Room

Other Titles from Miami University Press

Poetry Series

General Editor: James Reiss

The Bridge of Sighs, Steve Orlen
People Live, They Have Lives, Hugh Seidman
This Perfect Life, Kate Knapp Johnson
The Dirt, Nance Van Winckel
Moon Go Away, I Don't Love You No More, Jim Simmerman
Selected Poems: 1965-1995, Hugh Seidman
Neither World, Ralph Angel
Now, Judith Baumel
Long Distance, Aleda Shirley
What Wind Will Do, Debra Bruce
Kisses, Steve Orlen
Brilliant Windows, Larry Kramer
After a Spell, Nance Van Winckel
Kingdom Come, Jim Simmerman
Dark Summer, Molly Bendall
The Disappearing Town, John Drury
Wind Somewhere, and Shade, Kate Knapp Johnson
The Printer's Error, Aaron Fogel
Gender Studies, Jeffrey Skinner
Ariadne's Island, Molly Bendall
Burning the Aspern Papers, John Drury
Beside Ourselves, Nance Van Winckel

General Editor: Keith Tuma

Rainbow Darkness: an anthology of African American poetry, edited by Keith Tuma

Fiction Series

Edited by the Creative Writing Faculty of Miami University

Mayor of the Roses, Marianne Villanueva

the Waiting Room

by Albert Sgambati

Miami University Press
Oxford, Ohio

Library of Congress Cataloging-in-Publication Data

Sgambati, Albert, 1956-
The waiting room / by Albert Sgambati.
p. cm. – (The Miami University Press fiction series)
ISBN 1-881163-48-2 (9781881163480)
I. Title. II. Series.
PS3619.G36W35 2006
811'.6--dc22 2006012446

Many thanks to Kurt Lipschutz for his invaluable advice
and unflagging encouragement,
and to Laurie Price for her long years of support.

People count up the faults of those who keep them waiting.
—French Proverb

Contents

the Waiting Room

Life as an Afterthought

Shit. Rain. I flicked the switch on the Mr. Coffee coffee machine and remembered reading somewhere that a kid walked up to Joe DiMaggio on a plane and said, "Mr. Coffee, can I have your autograph?" It was almost nine. I'd slept late the way I imagined Marilyn Monroe had done. I watched the coffee pour into the glass pot. The calibrated marker silk-screened onto its side said six cups but the pot really held only two HEY WAKE UP! Walgreens mugs. Maybe that was one reason my marriage didn't work out. My plans to go out to the ballpark were blown too, but that was on account of the rain. I bought tickets when I still had a job and planned to play hooky from it. Now there was no need. Which had nothing to do with the rain. There was no game—apart from a wife or a job. It was a good thing there were no children, despite my ex-wife's desire for them. I dumped the wet grinds into the garbage under the sink and put in a new paper filter.

The phone rang and I picked it up to hear a click just as I was saying hello. I couldn't stop myself. Maybe they called for the same reason. The coffee was bringing me back into myself and I remembered my wife saying, "I don't understand you," and for the first time, sitting there sipping my coffee, I thought I understood.

I switched on the TV then walked back into the kitchen to refill the Mr. Coffee coffee machine humming "Dobie, Dobie, Dobie." Outside was as grey as a cat would see it. There was an open bag of Stella D'oro and I still had half a pack of cigarettes. The rain is good for plants and things, fish get to sleep. Sometimes I could be sort of content. A guy cracked an egg open and said, "This is your brain." As I stood waiting for the coffee I could tell just by listening that it was the episode where Dobie leaves the family grocery store to work at a soda fountain and Mr. Gillis hires Maynard.

To celebrate, I decided to flip some eggs and sip a whiskey. Tony the Tiger was smiling as I went to fetch the bottle. The phone rang halfway between Johnnie Walker and Tony the Tiger and I picked it up saying "Hello," while Tony said, "They're Gr-r-reat!"

"Bishop to black queen's four," said the voice at the other end.

"O.K.," I answered, scribbling it down on my cigarette pack.

"You're fucked now," he said and hung up.

When the coffee was ready I settled in, imagining an outfielder riding a cable car with his wife in the rain. Maynard was taking Dobie's place in the Gillis family, Dobie was hurt. Mr. G was also hurt, but they were both too proud to give into one another. I shut my eyes and listened. When I opened them Beaver was up in a tree, and later, the captain and the professor were beginning to boil in a large pot. I turned off the TV when I finally woke up to pee. *My Mother The Car*.

Somewhere someone in the building was listening to Judy Garland. I took a swallow of cold coffee. The phone rang and I picked it up thinking it was the most phone calls I'd gotten since the garage sale misprint.

"Hello," I answered like an AT&T operator on a double shift.

"Marvin?"

"You've got the wrong number."

Judy Garland was singing "Ding, ding, ding went the bell."

"Sorry," she garbled into the mouthpiece before the phone fumbled back into its cradle.

I was beside myself and it was time for a little nip. It was getting dark and I could hear the rain. Lotte Lenya had replaced Judy Garland and was singing "mit 'nem Messer in der Brust." My favorite part of the day.

I pulled back the curtains and sat there with a tumbler in my hand watching the rain and drinking from a bottle my boss had given me as a Christmas present. I didn't know what else to do. The job was beside the point. I paid my way by wit and stealth. Public education and the gene pool combined in a satiric twist to pay bills and rent with a little leisure time left over. Capitalizing on what a pediatrician once termed aphasic tendencies, I took the childhood disability directly to the public and they adored me for it.

Employing a low retaining wall at an entrance to Union Square as my pedestal, I froze, firmly, unaffected and resolute as a motionless presence, a repository for small change. Stock-still, painted and posed, I sold the silent places inside of me as a street artist. Earlier, I had done a series of jerky, mechanized gestures like a century-old wind-up wooden toy, for a quarter, but had long since removed the key from my back and rubbed away the red circles on my cheeks. Instead, I simply stood there, immobilized and unmoving.

Then there was the real work.

A life by vicarious means I had begun because of a girl named Lisa back in college, whom I followed all the way from French into the Oceanic language groups before she suddenly decided to move to Oregon. Like a cryptogram, my career had been launched.

As I poured myself another few fingers of Yuletide cheer I was beginning to feel like someone else—the way I like to feel. It was like my life in translation.

The next whiskey went down like water in a rainstorm, which it was.

My continuing work in translation was extra money, but that wasn't what was important about it. It was the

Sayama Heavy Industries–Hermanos Jimenez account I stole from my last employer that I coveted. That's what had brought us together. On a firmament of facsimile and FedEx, we came into contact. After years of labor, I finally found someone who knew the code once you peeled back the text. An unconscious search through all the stacks of hurried translations, business correspondence, product service manuals, travel guides and hotel brochures eventually led me to the abstracted edges of inner space where we met. She was someone who understood the caul of language with its obscure integument of words and quilted meanings. The Sayama Heavy Industries translator, or Sayama, as I called her, was that person. She spoke six languages and was working on a translation of Persian poetry into Japanese. We faxed our warm embraces.

At first, our mutual interest in Lepidoptera enhanced our association. After our contact developed into something more personal, I received specimens of a Death's Head Sphinx and a Birdwing from a Philippine rain forest. Then, when we discovered our oddly matched circumstances, her not being able to have children and my not wanting them, which accounted for the demise of our respective marriages, we were drawn even closer.

At seven o'clock the next morning, the sun pasted itself on the windowpane like a fried egg in a spattering pan. I guess I had done a little drinking the night before. There was an atlas, a Kurdish-English dictionary and a Bible on the floor next to me. I guess I had done a little reading, too.

Feeling my way to the kitchen, I dumped the moist grounds into the garbage and put a new filter and some fresh coffee into my Mr. Coffee coffee machine.

On TV, the Challenger was being piggybacked across a runway and a crowd of people waved little flags as it went by. Everything moved in waves. A cook in a shiny studio kitchen spoke of stew's unfair reputation. My head was pounding; time to go back to sleep.

I dreamed I was shoe-shopping with my ex-wife. A Latin guy cupped his hands below her ankle and looked up her dress. She touched him on the head and he asked her, "Cash or charge?" A twenty-first century dream. I woke up anxious with my head still pounding, wrote down my dream and went back to sleep.

The phone rang. I picked it up without opening my eyes. "No one is home right now. If you wish to leave a message you may do so at the tone." I walked to the front door with the phone, opened it, reached around the frame and pushed the buzzer. "Marvin please call," said the woman on the other end and hung up. My neighbor had just stepped from the elevator. He forced a little smile, which meant it must be around six or seven o'clock. I nodded and shut the door. My headache was gone. I walked to the kitchen thinking about the dream, hoping I'd written it down and not just dreamed I did—which I sometimes did. It suddenly occurred to me today was the next day. Life moves fast as an afterthought.

The phone was ringing again as I was attaching my clerical collar—a leftover from my marriage; that, and the policeman's uniform. I didn't pick up.

A Double Leo

The supermarket was crowded and smelled of wet dogs on rainy days. I had a sudden urge for Chinese food. The cashier called me "Father" and allowed me to cash a check without a second piece of identification. "God bless you," I said at the end of the transaction. Outside, a man with a bucket hanging from an aluminum tripod rang a bell and called out, "Help the needy," and "God bless you." We nodded at each other in a gesture of complicity as I walked by with my cello-bag on the way to dinner. If the streets weren't so crowded, it might have been possible to feel at one with the world.

I thought about Japan while picking through mung beans with red plastic chopsticks. I daydreamed butterflies and simultaneous interpreting. Everything breaks off into monosyllables, baby speech, utterances, clear and direct. I point to a fruit and smile, a woman holds up three fingers and I nod—it's happened before. I remembered wandering the streets of Saigon, then I imagined reciting Pessoa to Sayama in a Ginza song bar. It was something I was going to have to work on. Make the words mean what they said.

I decided on a drink before heading back home and stopped in at a local establishment distinguished by blinking red lights that edged the front window.

"What'll you have, Father?" the barman asked.

"Bourbon, neat."

"Make it two," the severely cropped, fiercely pierced redhead sitting on the stool next to me snapped while twisting an empty cigarette pack in her hands.

I held out one of mine.

"Thanks," she leaned towards me, waiting for a light. "You a regular?"

"No, I just stopped in. The rain makes me nostalgic."

"For booze?"

"No." She made me laugh.

"I didn't think you were much of a drinker," she squinted, meaningfully, "you know."

"Don't be fooled. Beer backs," I said when the barman put down the drinks. "Do you frequent this establishment?"

"Nah, I was just walking by and needed a drink."

"Do you do that often?"

"Only when I need a drink."

I held out my glass. "To need."

She toasted, "Nostalgia."

A few hours later, we were walking up over the hill not worrying about the rain. The barman said he'd catch up with us after he closed and counted out the register. I wrote my ex-wife's address on a pack of matches and handed it to him.

"I really appreciate you walking me home."

"It's closer than mine," she said. "I thought you guys lived in orders or dynasties or something."

"I'm a special case."

"You sure are."

"One of the chosen."

"Right again."

It dawned on me that I was being sexually objectified. A priest picked up by a ritually scarred punker—"A double Leo" she told me. And it seemed like we were in for a night if our legs could still carry us that far. I would have to forego my appointment with Sayama, though she would understand, or at least she wouldn't ask too many questions, the way my ex-wife always did.

I only really woke up the following morning when I stepped under the shower and reached for the soap-on-a-rope. It had been a present from my ex-wife and had outlasted our marriage. When she gave it to me she told me it was a joke. I laughed. Anything to please her. Once she gave me a blow dryer with a styling comb attachment. That was supposed to be a serious gift. There was no telling.

I found a note by the Mr. Coffee coffee machine that said, "I couldn't figure it out and there's a donut shop anyway on the corner thanks." With punctuation I would have been able to tell what she was talking about but it wouldn't have made a difference. I put my jacket on.

She was sitting at the counter that faced the street chewing on a cinnamon twist with a jumbo coffee in front of her, reading a newspaper. I walked into the second-hand clothing store kitty-corner and watched her turn the pages and brush crumbs away. When she finished, she took out a cigarette and stared out the window, sipping from her Styrofoam cup. Her skin was so light she lit up, and with the white cup in her hand, her red hair, and the sun, she seemed all aglow. I was reminded of the Christmas whiskey and the shark's tooth she had hanging by a chain from her neck.

She walked out onto Polk Street and headed towards Civic Center. I gave her half a block, then placed the broad-striped linen back in its bin and walked out the door. I lingered on a corner while she went into a bookstore, and when she came out ten minutes later she was carrying a small rectangular box—a deck of tarot cards, I guessed. I followed her all the way to Mission Street until she got on a bus and disappeared with the afternoon traffic, like fleeting moments that collect in the sentient heart of being. Loss became gain as the vanishing world was the very thing that pushed me forward. A last lonely glimmer transporting the memory of a one-night stand out of my life forever. I added a double Leo to the list.

Myself in the Place of Avocados

In good weather, there were sure to be enough tourists to make it worth my while. I stopped home and got my working gear together, painted my face and hands gold, sprayed my hair, and put on my gold metallic shirt, pants and shoes and headed down to the Square. There I sat, on the cornerstone by the steps leading up one side of the Square without moving, my big golden top hat at my foot, for a few hours.

People often comment on the difficulty of maintaining the statue-like pose for any length of time, but really nothing is further from the truth. Yes, it does take practice, but in the end it isn't much different from daydreaming out the window in grade school. There, on the concrete slab I lost all sensation of my body while my mind floated away. Sometimes the only thing that brought me back was the clinking of the coins falling into my hat.

With my pockets full from a Japanese tour bus, I walked back up Geary thinking of Sayama. After I was laid off, she managed to get me the Hermanos Jimenez account that I had handled for the last two years. I didn't even know her real name, or what she looked like; it didn't matter. I was at my computer some mornings by six o'clock and we made love in Mali and Mandarin from halfway around the world. She had scanned a photo of herself and told me I could click on her (fictitious) name, but I was afraid to destroy the image I had created in my mind with a press of the button.

I picked up my pace when I turned the corner at Larkin. Someone was following. I could feel it at my back. A gilded man in a fleshy world makes an easy target. I expected a hand to reach from behind and pull me down at any moment. They were close. I broke into a trot. The soft-shoe sound of padded fours hitting the ground with a galloping rhythm continued. When I figured out what it was I stopped and turned around. A haggard gray schnauzer kept its distance at about four feet and barked—conversationally. I listened for a few seconds then continued on my way. A few moments later, the schnauzer trotted past as I turned onto my street.

The phone was ringing. I remembered the bishop threatening my flank and decided not to pick it up. Then I remembered it was Saturday. My mother's weekly call. I pictured her on the balcony of her condo overlooking the Intercoastal Canal, listening to the phone ring on the other end. It's tough being an only child but, despite the pressure,

I didn't answer. I sat at my computer with a peanut butter sandwich and a cup of coffee. I knew Sayama had probably already gone to bed, but I checked the chat room where we usually met. Then, I checked my mail to find my mother's message from a couple of minutes prior, probably right after the phone rang.

"I'm alive and in Florida," it began. My heart sank. It was my fault for pushing her to get electronic mail so that we could "keep in touch." I had thought that it was a way to diplomatically curtail the requisite Saturday call, but now, instead, I was obligated to answer her frequent mail as well as take the weekly call.

I dialed her number.

"So, you think you can hide," she said.

"I was walking in the door when the phone stopped ringing. How are you?"

"Neglected and anemic from all the mosquitoes… other than that, fine."

Her anger, I knew, had something to do with my brother's death; she had never much complained before. It was difficult to put the pieces together because the size and shape of the puzzle kept changing. I didn't dare tell her about my position as a statue in Union Square. My divorce and loss of steady employment had compounded her worries, and telling her about my golden opportunity would only add to her anxiety.

Omission had already become the centerpiece in our relationship. I knew my refusal to speak about my brother confused her, but after he took up with the woman I'd planned to marry, years back, our already strained relationship collapsed. It wasn't until he was dead that she noticed anything amiss, but that was a topic I could hardly breach with my mother. Now he was gone. The police report said possible suicide, and I still held a grudge.

When I went overseas, everything seemed to recede with distance and, just about the time it disappeared, I returned. Then, with his death, he did it again, bringing that added tension back into my life. On top of a failed marriage and bitter memories, I was now my mother's only child, thanks to him, and a puzzling one at that. He, not I, had been our mother's son.

Nothing had ever been easy between my mother and me. I remembered her asking me years back, "Is there any money in Urdu?" and I couldn't really answer her—explain how the words broke apart. I had been visiting her in Florida, finishing my thesis on Dogo dialects, when the man with the paisley tie from the job fair called. We went to the supermarket for lobster to celebrate. She stood over the avocados and said, "My, these are very dear," like they were orphaned children. Little did I know that years later I would see myself in place of those avocados.

If things were different, I might have been someplace else right then, but I felt I owed it to her to at least be in the same country, even if I failed at babies, marriages and mortgages. For her they were what existence amounted to, and I imagined that when my brother was alive she had company in those feelings. Now, I suspected the emptiness of her life was somehow, in her mind, reflected in mine. Sometimes I thought about the time when I'd worked in Asia and Africa, before my brother died, prior to when I knew my ex-wife, and I longed for those days.

I thought of my mother, alone, under a fluorescent light, peeling potatoes into a stainless steel sink.

Three Jeans

The previous night was beginning to catch up and I needed a drink or some rest, maybe both. Whatever I did, I wanted to be up the following morning to talk with Sayama. As her marriage began crashing, I became an important part of her life. Her inability to have children severely cut into her worth as a wife and permitted her husband the right to pursue other women, which he did with a disregard that, in my opinion, was unwarranted. The issue of divorce, unless he brought it up, was non-existent. So it was on this plane of alienation and loss that we first found common ground. As our relationship developed, that territory broadened, pushing at its borders until she had become the most important person in my life.

I poured myself a brandy and soda and turned on the television. The Discovery Channel was airing a program about an Arctic expedition; three men were crossing the Bering Strait on foot in the dead of winter. They were French and the narrator was doing all the voice-overs. Their names were Jean-Michele, Jean-Paul and Jean-Marie. I thought of the Third Republic. At the end of the show, they arrive at a tiny village on the outer reaches of some windswept peninsula in Alaska where one of the Jeans pulls a bottle of champagne from his pack and they make a toast.

The phone rang. I picked it up and walked to my front door and opened it while answering, "No one is home right now. If you wish to leave a message you may do so at the tone," then reached around the frame and pushed the buzzer. "Marvin please call," said a woman on the other end. There was a long pause, I cupped the receiver with my hand and imagined holding someone's chin between my thumb and forefinger before she said, "I'll be home all night," and hung up.

The three Frenchmen circled the village in a Piper Cub waving to a lone Eskimo in a field of white who waved back as if he were cleaning an enormous windshield. I wondered if the bartender ever caught up with my ex-wife, and poured myself another drink.

The evening was hopeless, but it made me giggle anyway. I downed my drink in a single swallow then went to the closet and got out my policeman's uniform, deciding I would freshen up with a shower. The scalding hot water felt good on my body, it lifted me out of a stupor I didn't even know I was in. I found the wire-frame mirrored sunglasses in the top dresser drawer and put them on before walking out.

The schnauzer picked me up at the corner. I caught him out of the corner of my eye running from between two parked cars. A Citroën and a Peugeot. I thought of Catherine Deneuve in *The Last Metro*. The schnauzer kept its distance.

At the Vietnamese place on the edge of the Tenderloin, I ripped through three of those paper-thin steaks and a salad dressed in sugar and red food coloring. A black coffee, lightened and sweetened with Carnation evaporated milk was the perfect ending to a perfect meal. The schnauzer jogged past the plate glass window. Things were suddenly looking up. I still had a few hours to kill before I could be with Sayama so I decided to walk down to the Mission District for a drink.

There was a place with a good juke and a pool table on the corner of Capp and Seventeenth. It was always fun setting an example as to where officers of the law could create the most indelible impressions. The receptions are always interesting, some places clear out, and in others, everybody wants to buy you a drink—in this place people were too self-conscious to do either. It was just my speed.

A Willy Kind of Day

The bartender knew he should have carded the three girls huddled together at the corner table but instead turned a blind eye. He recognized them from the neighborhood, and besides, he was busy and the place was so crowded no one would notice.

"With this," said one of the girls at the table showing the others the .38 stuffed into her purse.

"Don't do it, Marie," her friend sitting next to her advised. "It'll make more trouble than it's worth."

"What do you expect me to do?"

"Get a restraining order," the girl sitting across from her said.

"Yeah, right," she answered shaking her head.

"Shit," the bartender grumbled when a cop walked through the door.

• • •

A few hours later, I was sharing a booth with three underage girls who all went to the same Catholic school around the corner. They were quite drunk and so was I, but nobody could tell anything because of the mirrored glasses. We made fun of the black stretch and leather crowd that tried hard not to look at us. I didn't have a gun, but the cuffs were threatening enough. The girls all called me officer and I called all of them Marie, since their names were Mariel, Mary and Marie. I told them the story about my arctic adventure with three men named Jean, right up until the waving Eskimo.

By one o'clock, two of the Maries had little red lines breaking through the roof of the Department of Motor Vehicle's safety limit graph and I offered to get them home before things got too sloppy. After all, I was a cop.

I pushed a couple of Maries out of the cab towards their front doors and asked the third one, the real (and only coherent) Marie where she wanted to go.

"I don't know, take me to the station."

"How about home?"

"If it's yours."

I gave the driver my address.

There are times when you need to stop and ask yourself what you're doing, and this was one of them, but I forgot the question as soon as I thought it. When we pulled up to my building the driver said, "Have a good night," just the way he shouldn't have.

After we got upstairs, Marie began fingering the cuffs hanging from my belt. When she got down on her knees and licked them, there was no doubt in my mind what she was hinting at.

It was a Sunday morning and when I got up I would rather have not had anyone there. I put on the coffee and had a drink as I cursed myself for having stood Sayama up two nights running. Marie lay oblivious in my bed, wrapped up in the covers she pulled off me during the night. I considered moving up my pawn. I was losing control, but there was nowhere else to go.

I would have cooked something if I didn't think the smell of food would wake her up and prolong the visit, and just as I was thinking it I heard her voice: "Hey what's for breakfast?"

"What do you feel like?"

"Shit. But if you could throw something together I'd sure appreciate it."

I heard the bathroom door shut, and about a minute later, the shower went on.

Pancakes. Just add water. Makes 8-12 servings. Right as I was discovering there was no syrup she rounded the corner and stood there, gangly, in the door, a pajama top barely clinging to her thin frame, like a Fruit of the Loom commercial with a hangover.

"We're out of syrup," I said.

"You might as well get the paper while you're down there."

I didn't argue. The morning was hopelessly lost already and I could use the fresh air. I walked past her into the bedroom and pulled a sweatshirt over my head.

"Do you want me to watch the pancakes?" she asked, as I brushed past her still standing in the doorway, on my way out.

"Do you believe in God?"

"No."

"Then watch the pancakes," I said, shutting the door.

She began to irritate me around the seventh inning. The Giants were away at Atlanta and it was a pitching duel you knew the Giants were going to blow, which made it all the more intense with everything leading up to that moment when all those talks on the mound and head shaking and kicking up dust wouldn't amount to anything. It was the kind of game that when someone walks everybody gets nervous.

"They're gonna blow it. Fucking Giants suck," Marie said to the screen like a true fan.

"Listen, I gotta get ready to go out," I said trying to prompt her.

"Do you mind if I stay here a while?" she asked, leaning over, the ends of her jet-black hair touching me on the shoulder.

"Yeah . . . okay," I said, only because I couldn't think of anything else. Then I got my things together without really having anywhere to go. A girl, who by daylight, looked more and more like a convincing case for statutory rape, was kicking me out of my home through my own stupidity. As soon as the door shut behind me I began to worry, leaving my apartment to a practically unknown teenage atheist who had invited herself into my bed, sort of.

• • •

Marie picked up the phone as soon as he had gone. "Mariel," she said, "this is perfect."

• • •

I thought it would be better to stick close by, just in case. I could go and sit at the donut shop for a while, and from there keep an eye on things. I picked out an old-fashioned and a lemon-filled as companions to a jumbo cup of java, before grabbing a discarded Sunday supplement that had disassembled itself across the seat in one of the booths specially designed for discomfort. The idea was to promote speed and efficiency and discourage the anti-capitalist concept of loitering. I often wondered about the donut shop strategy because it failed so miserably. Usually anybody with their wits about them or a mind in half-working order could only take a few minutes astride the oil byproduct seating units, though it wasn't uncommon for the booths to be taken up by families of one, arguing or furiously twisting napkins into the wee hours of the morning. Passenger comfort didn't seem to be an issue on their train at all.

As always, I took one of the stools in the corner with the plate glass windows facing out onto the street. I read William Buckley, William Safire and the little sidebar that held the witticisms of Will Rogers, just to make it a Willy kind of day.

Three Jeans, three Maries and now three Willies. Utterances. Jean–Marie–William, I thought, while sucking the lemon guck from the little hole in the side of the donut. I wondered if Marie was rifling through my drawers. She seemed the type. I had another few slugs of joe left and sipped slowly, taking the constantly forming Styrofoam film that looks like an oil slick right off the top with each slurp, wondering where to go next.

The King's Rook's Pawn

"What are you doing home so soon?" she asked as I came through the door. I didn't answer, and she sat there filing her nails and continuing to watch the television. It was a sunny afternoon, with the west coast game in the fourth inning and light pouring over the set in such a way that sometimes you could only see the wall and window reflected across the screen instead of the Padres and Pirates at Jack Murphy Stadium. I got a beer. The names of things will make you do that. I might have had something else but as soon as I heard "Jack Murphy" from the two-inch speaker my mind was made up.

Marie looked like Marie sitting on the couch; if I thought of a name like Alexander Hamilton I knew he was tall just by his name, Lincoln too. But Jack Murphy was with Jerry at the bar complaining. Sometimes I'd even watch the Dodgers just so I wouldn't have to hear the announcer say, "Here we are at Jack Murphy Stadium," and give in to the urge to grab a cold aluminum can from the refrigerator.

At times, language makes me wince.

What I had always thought of as shuddering phrases had long ago honed my interest in the mystery of phonemes and morphemes. I remembered that somewhere in my studies I began to question the logic of the system which mistook itself for logic itself. I slowly began to realize that we tended to box the language as pure Aristotelian classification, not as a method to test the meaning of our utterances against, but as a be-all and end-all of meaning itself. We compromised the inherent esotericism of linguistics for something we termed clarity, which really meant we carved it into a streamlined shape to transport the cargo of commerce more efficiently. We conceded its power to placate ourselves. Still, despite our taming of speech, even the biggest dullard of an accountant or computer programmer was driven to bristle once in a while.

I remember choosing Miles Standish over John Smith in a first-grade play, refusing to attach myself to the flattest name in the English language, a star route across the Kansas of Anglo imagination. I started to throw a tantrum so the teacher gave in—Miles Standish is another tall name. "We are happy to be here," I said to Rosa Dario and Richard Porkner, both dressed as Indians.

"You got another beer?" Marie asked.

I twisted a can off the plastic ring and gave it to her without saying anything. It was starting to get strange;

most women leave quickly, they peck at you with pursed lips like nothing ever happened and walk out, but Marie wasn't even dressed yet, and she didn't look like she was ready to go anywhere.

"You're not a real cop," she said suddenly.

"No, I'm not."

"Do you usually dress like that?"

"No, not usually."

"Oh," she said, and turned back towards the television.

I decided the best thing to do was ignore her—maybe she would just go away. I went into the bedroom, took off my shoes, turned on the portable Panasonic to Jack Murphy Stadium and lay down on the bed. The announcer said, "We'll be right back from Jack Murphy Stadium, here in San Diego."

The next thing I knew, she was pushing my shoulder like she wanted me to get up until I realized all she wanted was for me to move over so she could lie down. My body tightened and then suddenly bolted itself upright. I looked over at the clock and seeing that it was seven grabbed a sweatshirt and sat down at my desk to turn on my computer.

"Are you here?" I asked, as soon as I got in.

"Put your hands behind your back," she told me.

After that Sayama closed a pair of cuffs around my wrists and pushed me to my knees. She said she was angry that I hadn't told her I wouldn't be there the night before while twisting my nipples between her fingers. She sat on the chair in front of me, hiked up her skirt and berated me while she fingered her sex a few inches from my face.

Marie, whom I had forgotten about, was walking out of the kitchen with a cup of coffee in her hand when I finally got up from my desk.

"Want some?" she asked.

"Yeah… thanks."

I sat down at the small table in the kitchen while she poured my coffee.

"Don't you have to go to school?" I asked her.

"Not if I don't want to. Why are you worrying about it?" she asked, lowering herself onto my lap until she was straddling me and reaching under my sweatshirt.

There was nothing more to say as she closed tightly around me, moaning, grabbing the edge of the chair. I cupped the smooth, rounded curve of her in my hands. When we finished she kissed me. Right between the legs. And then poured us two fresh cups of coffee.

"How old are you?" I asked.

"Don't worry."

"I am."

"I'm not," she said.

"I could get into a lot of trouble."

She shrugged.

"And won't your parents be worried?"

She shrugged again.

We sat in silence sipping our coffees. I didn't know what else to say. Something had to be done but I was at a loss. The only thing I was sure of was that I had to stop the bishop from controlling the game. I lifted myself out of my chair, walked into the living room, picked up the phone and dialed. "I'm putting the king's rook's pawn up two," I told him.

"It took you long enough to decide you couldn't do anything else. My knight comes up right behind the bishop," he said, then hung up without a goodbye.

I stood there in the middle of the living room, stumped. Marie sat in the kitchen drinking coffee, flipping through the pages of a department store catalog without any sign of moving. I realized I wouldn't have needed to go anywhere if she would just leave, but arguing seemed futile. I picked up the parcel of butterflies I had made up for Sayama, a Prima Orangetip and one of the most beautiful Pearly Marbles I had ever seen, and headed for the door.

Home

After the post office, I headed over to the library in Civic Center. Aside from my home, the library and museum were my only other places of asylum. These types of refuge, once common, have become increasingly scarce. Maybe because they're without any real function, a sort of limbo or crack marring the illusion of harmony promised by production and consumption. And really, that is exactly the charm of a library, hidden knowledge that reflects a state of being. That, along with art, cordoned off and awarded the same status as Mount McKinley, are some of the few public spaces where you can glimpse the high unreachable corners—refuge, sentiment, essence, memory—call it what you like—and that's where I found myself once again.

I wandered the long solid aisles. The stacks were a ghost town. A man with a volume of Martin Buber was eating from a Wonder Bread bag. *Forgotten America* was on the floor. Where the ceiling changed to wire mesh you could see the people upstairs as they combed obituaries for the names of relatives, lovers, old enemies. And underneath, little boys were bursting with folders and leaky thermoses probing for hard facts—the latitude of New Zealand, the capital of Idaho—at the information desk.

I picked a book up off a shelf and began to read:

> *We must not forget that an object is the best messenger of a world above that of nature: one can easily see in an object at once a perfection and an absence of origin, a closure of brilliance, a transformation of life into matter …*

I walked home feeling a little more at ease with myself. A group of men sat against a concrete retaining wall passing a bottle. On the other side of the fence some Vietnamese kids hit a rock back and forth with the broken pieces of a broomstick, and a skinny teen-ager said, "Blowjob ten dollars," as I walked by.

My head was full. I wanted to talk to Sayama in the worst way.

"Check it out," Marie said as I opened the door. She was sitting on the sofa in front of the television with a can of beer. I walked over, pulled off my sweatshirt, and sat down. Rescue people, law enforcement and reporters were gathered around a well.

"What's going on?" I asked.

"There's a little girl stuck down there."

"Stuck?"

"Since yesterday. Right now they don't know if she's just sleeping or dead. The Red Cross just threw down peanut butter sandwiches and grape Kool-Aid."

I had an enjoyable evening with Marie despite the situation. The high drama of real life broadcast and beer charged the moment. Sometime after midnight the little girl was pulled to safety on a sort of sling that closed over her as she stepped in. The first thing she must have seen when back up on the surface were lights from television cameras. You could see that she'd wet her pants, though this wasn't mentioned during the broadcast. When they pushed the microphones at her she whined, "Mommy." It was a perfect television moment but we really didn't pay much attention.

When I woke up Marie was drooling on the pillow. It was six o'clock and Sayama wasn't on yet. I decided to make some coffee. Nina Simone sang about a "beat-up little seagull," as the Mr. Coffee coffee machine burned its resinous drippings to brown smoke on the aluminum-plated heating coil. It was that part of the day when homeowners in striped pajamas stretched in their doorways. Birds were singing. In a couple of hours every major route into the city would be jammed, helicopters would fly over jackknifed trailers, and reality would be collaged together in network newsrooms and it would all make sense.

I carried the steaming HEY WAKE UP! Walgreens mug into the bedroom and sat down in front of the screen. Marie opened her eyes for a second, grabbed the covers, turned over and went back to sleep. When I looked up, I saw that Sayama had her hands tied to the bedpost and was bent over at the waist. I came up from behind as she groaned somewhere between resistance and pleasure.

Afterwards, Sayama told me that her husband, coming home drunk the night before, had threatened her again. She deflected, as always, my suggestion of leaving for her own safety. The situation, which would be termed "classic" by some psychologists, was already familiar to her in behavioral terms. She had read the books; what she wanted was someone to talk to. The two of us filled our conversations with wishes, all of them within the realm of possibility, though we never referred to them as such. It was like a balancing act on barbed wire. The edges were softened by imagination, our work, and those beautiful specimens seemingly frozen in flight: Swallowtails, Sulphurs, Orangetips, Whites, Hairstreaks and Blues. There, in that indefinable place that warped time and held no ground, there was evidence of real life.

Marie was coming out of the shower as I signed off. This was my other life. Pushing up pawns one square at a time in defense. I watched her dry her hair. I thought of my dead brother. It would have been a good day to go down to Union Square only I didn't feel like it.

I picked up my keys from the dresser and she asked, "Going out?"

"Yeah, for a walk."

"Wait up," she said, so I waited.

She had on a flight jacket and the knee-length bulk-knit sweater my sister-in-law was making for her boyfriend before he walked out on her and never came back, some sweatpants and Converse high-tops. She'd put on lipstick and tied a scarf, like the love interest on a Cuban trawler from a silver-edged classic, around her neck. I wanted to tell her she was a mirage and run my hands right through her.

The sky was a stone grey slate pressing upon us. Drivers turned on their headlights. We headed into the wind towards the bay. An Irish Setter chased a stick on the beach in Aquatic Park and we sat in silence. Marie tossed potato chips to the gulls. She put on a pair of headphones and rocked back and forth on the breaker, her legs tucked under her. I settled my head into the small space between her crotch and bended knees and slept.

An enormous glockenspiel with mechanical figures was set into motion by a clock as it struck the hour. "Cogs" was the word that came to mind and I was suddenly on the seashore watching a big white riverboat slowly sinking as it sent up two thick columns of smoke. My mouth was dry and the rolling surf misted over me as it pounded along the shore. When I opened my eyes it was drizzling. Marie looked down at me and said, "You were making sucking sounds."

Tiny drops of rain caught on my lashes and trimmed the world in diamonds and crystals as I squinted upward. She touched my hair. A stream of water rolled down my forehead, rounding the edges of my eyes until it dripped from my cheeks. She lit two cigarettes, giving one to me and cupping her hand over the other. I watched her fingers glow red around the burning ash. We walked back without saying a word. She put her arm around my waist and rested her head against my shoulder. It felt good and I was thinking I would like to make love with Marie right there under the rain in Aquatic Park.

When I left her at the front door to my building she stretched out her neck, kissed me on the cheek and walked inside. I wanted to be alone. There was a lot to think about. Blocking with my knight was the safest bet. Sayama sleeping somewhere on the outskirts of Tokyo. Then there was Marie. I bought a pack of Nat Shermans, walked up to the top of California Street, to the square in front of Grace Cathedral, sat down on a bench and lit up.

As the sun appeared two young boys beat each other with Styrofoam bats, one blue one and one red one. The woman who I assumed was their mother sat at the edge of the fountain calling out, "Don't hit too hard, Aaron."

A couple walked by, a tall skinny blond kid with a "Don't Waste It, It's The Only One We've Got," T-shirt, talking to an even skinnier Asian girl announcing, "Act Up!" and saying, "The average American is too stupid to understand." A man on a scooter with his dog in a basket turned onto California Street. I was enjoying my cigarette, watching people go in and out of the cathedral. The breeze was soft and wet, riding off the banks of fog that rolled slowly behind it, and it seemed incredible to me at that moment that the birds in the trees and the schnauzer tumbling in the grass, the sleeping drunk, the mailman and the can collector failed to pay it any mind.

The woman watching the two children got up, ambled over to me with her hands in her pockets and asked, "Do you have an extra cigarette?" then quickly added, "I'm trying to quit." Her hair fell at an angle that covered almost all of one eye. She spoke with a slight Slavic accent.

"Playing?" I motioned over to the children with my head, while taking out a cigarette for her.

"Positive aggression," she said. "I guess they have to get it out somehow, you know, without hurting anybody . . . break the circle of violence . . . something like that."

The kids were running around trying to pummel pigeons now that they were tired of clobbering each other. I envied them laughing at the escaping pigeons. We smoked our untreated slow-burning cigarettes, and it was kind of awkward and kind of comfortable at the same time.

"I really didn't need a cigarette, I was just curious what they were like," she said, holding out the thin black Nat Sherman in front of her. "They taste sort of funny."

"That's because they're expensive."

"Are you rich?"

It made me laugh a little. "No, just a splurge."

"I could do with some of that," she said.

Before I could comment, an old Oldsmobile Tornado, its left front fender hanging almost to the street in a grimace, pulled up and the driver, a muscle-bound guy in a sleeveless T-shirt and slicked-back hair leaned on the horn. Glaring at me, he yelled out the window, “Come on, Jeanette,” as she was grabbing the two children by the hand and getting them settled into the backseat. Then they fishtailed around the corner and out of sight.

• • •

“No, I haven’t seen them,” Marie answered.

“They’re all over the neighborhood, every laundromat and traffic light,” Mary said, as Mariel nodded in agreement, before adding, “like you’re wanted or something.”

“Why are they even bothering?” Marie asked.

“Well, whatever,” Mary said, “they’re making it clear they want you home.”

“Home,” she forced a laugh.

Two Big Bowls of Ramen

It was early evening when I returned to find the three Maries in my living room, one Marie brushed another Marie's hair, and the other Marie sat on the coffee table. An open bag of Cheese Doodles and a few long-necked bottles of beer completed the tableau. The phone rang and (my) Marie picked it up answering, "There's no Marvin here."

"It's Admiral Perry," said the hair-brushing Marie. And the other Marie (getting her hair brushed) said, "Good evening officer."

Startled by their presence, "Hi Marie," was the only thing I could manage to say.

I switched on the Mr. Coffee coffee machine, sat down at the table and thumbed through an old *National Geographic*. A Milwaukee spread: white picket fences and a cold harbor with a red brick factory in front reminded me of the towns I put together with my train set as a child.

Outside the window the fog was beginning to close in. The streetlights wore yellow halos. It would soon be dawn in Japan. The coming night was a "sh" sound drifting by. The TV clicked on and I heard Peter Jennings' voice and two Maries calling out, "Bye!" as they left.

I sat down on the sofa where Marie was already stretched out and picked up the phone, ready to make my next move. Suddenly, without warning, I was jarred. For a split second, I thought it was an earthquake and felt the fright strain in my chest as my heart skipped a beat. A blind-side blunt kick, spilled hot coffee over my wrist and forearm. Reacting, I threw what was left in my cup at her, which was luckily blocked from her face by a magazine. She was quick and came at me with her nails. I grasped her arms and scissored her legs between mine while holding her far enough away so she couldn't bite.

"What are you doing?"

"What's it to you?" she snapped.

Her eyeliner ran down the side of her nose and her cheek, then her arms collapsed under the pressure of my grip as she let herself fall forward, crying. I wanted to say something but didn't quite know what. "It's okay," I said finally, not knowing whether it was to comfort her or somehow address my own confusion.

At that moment, the phone began to ring. I picked it up and the woman on the other end said, "Marvin, it's you."

"I think you have the wrong number."

"Marvin don't…"

I hung up, not to be rude, just that there was something else to attend to at the moment.

"I liked when we were walking," Marie said.

"What?"

"This afternoon, when we went down to the bay. It felt good. Even after you left."

I simply nodded in agreement with what seemed to be a conversation already in progress.

"It was the first time in a long time I didn't feel so by myself," she continued. She looked up after a long pause. I waited for her to go on. "You know there are some things I just can't explain to you."

"Our life together," I said, trying to make light of it, "does seem a little confusing at times."

I went into the kitchen and put my cup in the sink. Then I walked back to the living room and poured myself a straight bourbon while turning on the television to watch the nightly news video clips of bug-eyed African children with bloated bellies and four-alarm fires in Oakland. Marie sat down with a glass of Tang and flipped through one of my ex's fashion magazines. She only looked up for the commercials, urgent sound bites laid over rapid-fire montages designed to make people look up from their magazines.

During the weather segment she asked me, "Don't you have any friends?"

I shrugged.

"I mean it seems like nobody ever comes around here or calls or anything."

"I just got over a divorce."

"So?"

"And…well, there's Sayama."

"Your girlfriend?" she asked, turning herself on the couch so she faced me.

"Yeah."

"Where is she?"

"In Japan."

"When's she coming back?"

"She lives there."

"Oh. When was the last time you saw her?"

"Well, I've never actually seen her, but we get together almost every day over the Internet."

She laughed, and then began asking me all sorts of questions.

"So will you ever meet?"

"We talk about it sometimes, but that's not the point."

"What is the point then?"

I watched the flashing images of women crying in Gaza, not knowing how to answer, and poured another bourbon. She waited as I sipped my drink. I didn't know what to tell her and she was making me uncomfortable. "Do you feel like going out for a walk?"

"Don't you ever feel lonely?" she asked as we walked up Van Ness and made the turn west on Geary.

"No," I answered.

"How's that possible?"

"I don't even have to put my mind to it."

All at once she turned towards me and placed a big wet kiss on my lips.

By the time we got to Japantown she was ecstatically rapping a popular tune with a chorus of: *so I hit my fuckin' bitch* down the echoing halls. While turning a corner in the surveillance-secured passageways, the wandering eyes of my ex hit me square on. She was sitting at one of the pagoda-covered picnic tables. Her glare pinned me to my creaking footsteps and a smirk slowly spread across her face. As if that weren't enough, I spotted the bartender, to whom I'd given the matchbook with her address, turning away from the automatic teller machine. Dazed, I slunk by. They sat across from each other picking shrimp and rice balls from waxed cardboard containers with balsa chopsticks. After the once-over she put her head down and concentrated on the soy-soaked mung beans. I hugged the far wall, put Marie between us, and became as small as I possibly could while we passed.

We ordered two big bowls of ramen, and tea that tasted like dirt. Marie wanted to see a movie but I was afraid. There was some kind of film festival going on, and knowing that my ex's idea of a perfect evening was dinner and a movie followed by some ritual alcohol and the missionary position, I suggested going home instead.

The One That Drowned

The following morning I went over translations with Sayama. There was an intimacy in the way we worked together. The mind/body split of every relation I had ever had didn't exist with her. We climaxed with the symbols on the outer reaches of memory, excavating Delphic utterances and rescuing them from the dead. We mined language as fertile pasture in an ethereal realm. If her barren womb was unable to produce mortal offspring it was more than compensated for by the shapes she produced with words, as they manifested themselves in a glistening chimera on the edge of some reality where we met.

We touched one another even while performing the most mundane tasks. Our territory was tempered by something ordinarily the provenance of poetry and religion. Our bodies, in a sense, floated, and our children were expression and annunciation, conjuring magic. She understood the banished tongue; our conversations skittered on a polyglot creole of borrowed phrases in which usage defied narrow rationale.

"Moo aki desu, je t'aime, immer nach sempre."

Turning off the computer I felt like a Russian space dog whose Sputnik had suddenly fallen from the sky. After a session with Sayama my equilibrium altered. I was home. I went into the kitchen and switched on the Mr. Coffee coffee machine. Backed once again into the small corner of my cosmos, I thought about Marie. It was time I put a stop to it. I hadn't mentioned her at all to Sayama and felt guilty about it. While it was true I liked Marie, I was afraid that the situation would lead to something I wasn't ready to deal with. Her age, as well as the fact that I had somehow been entrapped, made me feel justified in asking her to leave.

I sat down in front of the TV with my coffee and when Marie came out of the bathroom she had blond streaks in her hair and one of my flannel pajama tops stuffed into a pair of jeans. She crushed some cookies into a glass of milk, added a little coffee, and sat down next to me on the couch to watch the morning news.

"What do you do all day?" she asked. "Don't you have to go to work?"

"I have an appointment tonight," I told her, not even knowing why I said it. "And yes, I work, I'm mostly self-employed. And you?"

"Well, so far so good. I've been meaning to ask you about letting me keep things together for you, like I could do the dishes and the laundry and things while you're out working, or doing whatever."

"Marie, what's up with your parents? And school and…what's going on?"

"Hey, I don't go probing into your personal life."

"What? You're sleeping in my bed."

"So? What are you trying to say?"

"That things need to change."

"Well, I'm right here, so when things change, just let me know."

"You're probably in enough trouble as it is. Why do you want to make things even more complicated?"

She gave me a hard look.

"Marie, you're going to have to go," I said, as gently as I could manage.

"And if I don't?"

"There might be a problem."

"More than you can imagine."

"Oh?"

"Having sex with a minor, kidnapping, impersonating an officer of the law—off the top of my head, that's all I can think of right now."

All I could do was sit there and stare at her incredulously while she got up and walked into the bedroom, shutting the door behind her. I turned up the volume on the set so as not to hear her cry. When the phone rang I picked it up and didn't speak.

"Marvin?"

We were all somehow twisting ourselves into a knot.

"Please don't do this to me, Marvin."

I gently placed the receiver back into its cradle. When the phone rang again I reached down and pulled the plug from the wall.

I watched *Mr. Ed* without really paying much attention. What I really wanted to do was leave, but I felt like I needed to hold my ground. If I took drugs this probably would have been a good time to do them. But by three o'clock that afternoon I had, without realizing it, drunk myself into a semi-stupor. Marie hadn't left my bedroom since locking herself in that morning. I wanted to check my mail and get a fresh change of clothes.

The situation reminded me of living with my ex-wife. I'd often felt compelled to do something or act a certain way without being able to explain it to myself. It was something of an endurance test that had to do with pride. I remembered it going on for days.

Finally out of want of anything better to do, I made myself up and headed for Union Square. A few office workers coughed up some change but tourists were scarce. I hung my gaze on the panhandler who leaned himself up against a parking meter across Powell Street each day, holding a sign that read, "Have AIDS. Doing The Best I Can. Please Help."

When I got back home and opened the door to check on Marie she was sitting at the computer going through a search engine list. She turned around and asked me, "So how do you talk on this thing?"

I was surprised she had gotten that far but said nothing, went over to the machine and connected her to a sixty-channel location. I found a room called Dr. Calagari's Cabinet and typed in, "Hi everybody!!!" Mr. Pump responded, "Hi *Marie*," and JoyBoy, "Hello Marie. How old are you?:)"

She was typing something when I walked out with a change of clothes.

"This is kind of dumb," she said still sitting there, when I came back in after my shower.

"Sometimes," I said.

"I mean it's all right, one of these guys is from Taiwan, but I'd rather go out and see who I'm talking to or use the phone. It's weird."

"That's the idea, you have to use your imagination."

"Oh."

"Or get a camera."

I shut the door behind me and left Marie to her initiation into the virtual world. On the street I treated myself to a Happy Meal then lingered in a few of the used bookstores. Rounding a corner on the way home I noticed a sailor's uniform in the window of the second-hand clothing store. Sixteen dollars including the hat.

When I walked in Marie had the stereo turned up and was sitting at my computer in her underwear smoking a marijuana cigarette. She turned around as I entered the room and began to laugh, "Look, I already have a boyfriend. He's from Canada."

I went over to the screen and read Marie's last entry: "She unzips his pants and takes it in her hand. She begins to masturbate him until he becomes hard and then she gets down on her knees."

The response read: "Oh Marie, you're so good to me, you know exactly what I like."

"What do you think I should do now?" she asked me taking a drag off her cigarette.

"I don't know, use your imagination."

She put one hand on my crotch and typed in: "She feels him throbbing and takes it from her mouth waiting for him to..." with the other.

When I left the second time she was still at the computer, drinking a can of Coke. I was going to say something, but she was typing so furiously that I walked out of the room not wanting to disturb her.

I wandered over the hill towards North Beach in my freshly pressed Navy blues. A sailor is always well treated in a port town, and especially in San Francisco with its perverse affection for men in uniform.

I practiced my roll all the way to the bar, swaying from side to side. I already had a place on Columbus in mind. When I pushed through the door and barreled up to the bar the bartender asked me, as if on cue, "What'll ya have sailor?" Then a little later a guy at the urinal next to me said, "If you got nothing better to do why don't you walk over to my table."

Then he blushed and began to giggle, "Oh, no. It ain't what you think. You see my girlfriend's friend thinks you're cute. You'd be doing me a favor."

I was telling her about the South China Sea by the time her third Daiquiri came and she put her hand on my knee. When I suggested a stroll she grabbed me by the arm and we headed for the door. I hadn't paid the bill, but I figured since I was doing the guy a favor…

Around midnight I was pulling myself through the third-story window where she'd forgotten her keys. An old woman watched from across the way. The girl explained that she was locked out and my ship had just come in. She was planning on preparing my first home-cooked dinner in three months. I tumbled into her kitchen and landed on a crowded counter top. By the time I got downstairs she was holding herself up on the wooden rail with two hands.

The next morning walking home I couldn't help but feel a little bit ashamed of myself. It was confusing, especially under the circumstances. I thought about Marie and felt sorry for her. I sensed she somehow regarded herself a victim of an inane reality—pretty much as I did. Her inexplicable behavior, ultimately, made sense to me.

Then, for some reason, I remembered my brother telling me one of the last times I spoke to him, "You're not going anywhere. You think you're so fucking smart, but you'll see how far it's going to get you." And therein lay the argument. He had smashed into the only tree on a flat stretch of road at eighty miles per hour while I was still waiting for it to unfold. My wife and I had had a similar discussion. She always said things like, "Seize the day," while I felt the day was somehow tightening up around my throat.

As I climbed down the steps on the other side of the hill the taunting schnauzer popped out of some bushes and shadowed me through the streets.

I put some coffee in the Mr. Coffee coffee machine and stripped off my clothes. She was curled up asleep with the portable television still on. I left my uniform in a pile on the floor, grabbed a robe, and headed for the shower. As I was stepping from the bathroom Marie walked by in her panties and a sailor cap.

"So you were a sailor last night?" she asked, as I followed her into the kitchen and poured a cup of coffee.

"Yes, I was." I answered.

"What do you want?" she asked.

"What do you mean?"

"I mean, I don't understand. It's like you have no use for people other than amusement. I don't get your life."

I had to laugh. "Out of the mouths of babes."

"Don't give me that shit."

"I'm not. I think we're a little bit the same in some ways."

"Yeah?" She raised an eyebrow.

My stomach rumbled.

"We can talk about it over breakfast," I said, giving into the pangs of an overwhelming hunger after a night of drinking. "Let's get something to eat, my mouth tastes like dishwater."

We installed ourselves at the corner booth of a favorite greasy spoon with constant coffee that bestowed titles on their breakfasts like "The Hungry Farmer" and "Pig Heaven." The waitresses wore pink and the cash register had a pull-down handle. Years of cigarettes and rendered fat leant the locale an aroma that could only be described as seepage. It was atmospheric in a literal sense, had a certain pallor all its own.

"So tell me something about you," I asked after placing our order. "I hardly know anything about you."

"And we're already living together!" she laughed.

I waited.

"You first," she said.

"Anything you want to know."

"Tell me about your work."

"I'm a translator. I work from home."

Marie gave an assenting nod.

"And I also do some street performance."

She arched a brow over one eye. "Like a mime or a juggler?"

"Yeah, sort of."

"Sort of… what exactly do you do?"

"Well… I just stand there and don't move, like a statue."

She laughed. "That's perfect for you. In other words, you do nothing."

I nodded. "Now it's your turn."

"I'm not a good story teller," she said. "I don't know…"

"What's the best thing that ever happened to you?" I asked to prompt her.

"You sound like the religious instruction guy."

"Okay, the strangest, or just some odd thing that happened."

"Is this a quiz or something?"

"For ten points of your grade."

"Okay," she said, "this is a good one," as the waitress filled our cups. "I remember we had a picnic on Angel Island. It was about five years ago." Then she paused. "No, I can't. I feel stupid telling you this."

"C'mon," I prodded her on, "you already have my undivided attention."

"Alright." She screwed up her face. "But it's not a great story."

I waited, while she finished sipping her coffee, for her to begin.

"I don't remember why," she said, "but my whole family was there, cousins and friends. One of my uncles went walking on one of the beaches with two of my cousins. I think they had been drinking. Anyway, one of them bet my uncle he couldn't swim out to one of the buoys. My uncle, a real macho type, immediately stripped off his clothes and dove into the bay. In less then ten seconds he was being swept away by the undertow down the length of the island. My cousins tried to keep up on land but eventually lost sight of him."

"Drowned?"

"They came back to where we were having our picnic, and everyone went running. The Coast Guard was called and for a couple of hours we stood on the beach watching the cutter circle the island as a helicopter circled overhead."

"Quite a story," I said as the waitress put down our plates and filled our cups again.

"It was the last time I remember my whole family together. So where did you go last night?" she asked.

"You know, out."

"What's wrong, don't you even like me?"

I looked down at my plate. I could hear the hurt in her voice. It was a moment in which I could have said something, reassured her, but didn't.

"I'd do anything for you," she said, making me feel uncomfortable. "I don't have anything else, really."

"So did they have a funeral service?"

It was the worst thing I could have said. Tears began to stream down her cheeks. She shook her head, "I don't remember."

I left Marie at my front door. I didn't want it to go on and the only way I knew how to stop it, at least temporarily, was to shake myself loose and go off on my own.

When I got home that evening, there were candles burning in the living room, down the hall, even in the kitchen. Marie, wearing a short black pleated skirt and a white woven peasant blouse, came up to me like Donna Reed, and said, "Dinner's ready."

I sat down to rolled breast of chicken stuffed with proscuitto, olive paste and sun-dried tomatoes, a side of saffron rice and salad with mustard dressing. There was a bottle of wine already open. I heard myself predictably saying, "What's the occasion?" and stopped. I picked up my knife and cut into the chicken. Marie did the same. After filling our glasses we toasted and continued eating without a word. The entire meal passed in silence until the second bottle of wine. A Chenin Blanc.

"About six months ago, I was at a market," she said, after pouring the first glass. "One of those places where each stall is a separate business. I was only walking through because it's shorter than going all the way around the block, and as I was passing the section where they sell fish I saw my uncle."

"The one that drowned?"

"Yup."

"What! What did you do?"

"I just stood there looking at him. He saw me as he turned around. We stared at each other for a few seconds."

"And?"

"That's it."

"What did your family do?"

"I never told anyone—I was happy for him."

I laughed. It was wonderful. Marie got up to put on the coffee.

For some reason I thought of my ex right then and wondered what she was doing.

The Book of Change

After I put Marie to bed I sat at my computer and waited for Sayama. By six it was obvious she wasn't going to make it. I lit a cigarette, walked over to the stereo, flipped the switch and sat back down. The station played a variety of music I had previously thought was scored for department stores and supermarkets, though it produced its desired effect. I jumped out of my chair, snapped from a waking daze by the ringing phone.

"Hello?"

"You know, I never asked you why you waited until the burial to come," my mother said in her dry, crackling voice that reminded me how old she was. "I thought I already knew why, even if I couldn't put it into words."

"Well..." I said, and let a space fall between us.

"I don't know," she said. "I just thought I'd ask."

I could hear her crying. I could picture it. Her closed fist around a bit of tissue, covering up the mouthpiece. "Your brother was so good," she said. "I know you two had your problems..."

The call ended with the weather and news of a family I'd lost a lifetime ago. For a few seconds I sat there with the phone in my hand remembering Sunday dinners—my father, my mother, my brother and me sitting around the kitchen table—each detail that lived only in memory.

I pressed down the receiver and waited for the tone before dialing.

"Knight to queen four," I said.

"It's fuckin' six o'clock in the morning."

"And it's your move."

When I crawled into bed my brother haunted me all the way to my dreams.

I woke up that afternoon as a flurry of paper whizzed out of the fax machine into the tray. Marie was nowhere in sight. I went over to the machine and sifted through a translation Sayama had sent from her office. On the last page was a note that said she would be waiting for me tonight. I was ecstatic.

I could stay at home most of the week and work. Counting up the pages I figured that the one job would cover my rent and bills, and if I decided to work the Square it would be extra money.

I went to buy a can of coffee and a box of Devil Dogs before getting on with the job. It had been a while, and the prospect of digging into a translation excited me. I stopped for a pack of cigarettes then decided to sit in one of the cafés and treat myself to a pastry, a newspaper, and a breath of fresh air.

• • •

"What do you think you're doing?" the man said as he walked from behind the laundromat counter towards Marie.

She held up the flyer she had just taken down from the bulletin board next to her face and said, "They found the girl."

He nodded to Marie and she walked out, continuing up the street ripping her image from telephone poles and light posts.

• • •

As I turned the corner, exiting from the café, I caught sight of my ex-wife coming out of a florist shop, gladiolas wrapped in paper tucked under her arm. We stopped and stared at each other for a few seconds.

"So now you're baby-sitting to make a living," she said.

"No, I'm . . ."

"New girlfriend?" She raised an eyebrow and, without waiting for an answer, unlocked her car, got in, and drove off.

My whole life had come untied and my ex, in a moment both quirky and callous, had helped bring that fact to light. As before, she left me to dwell on the ever-wavering boundary between stability and the ethereal—in effect, a tally where the slim sum of my existence added up, just barely. I stood there, watching the fleeting gleam of sunlight off the chrome of her rear bumper, lost it to traffic and recalled years of wandering. With a small bag containing a laptop and modem, a cell phone and a couple of credit cards, I was able to carve a future from dealing with abstractions. A certain contentedness wrought from failing—the very thought of my brother penetrating my girlfriend which launched me into an otherness where I was finally able to define myself.

Before that, a life had been planned, one I still thought about from time to time. My ex-girlfriend had been the one to bring it up one drunken night in which no harm was meant, so she said. There, a knot had been tied along the rope of existence on which I stood, already shaken and unsteady. She was the one who would have delivered me from myself into the wider world. Slowly, she had gained my trust, culling an interest in the interior idiom that formed the island where I had taken refuge. With an eloquent simplicity, shaped by her easy manner and confidence, she had won me over.

Now they were gone—she and my brother. I remembered running away with a sudden and desperate fury, the English classes, work in newsrooms and offices, picking crops, tending bar, writing copy and translating documents, as if that previous life had all been someone else's.

When I met my wife, on a return trip from Asia to visit my mother, I sank easily into that dark, warm place where all life's mysteries reside in the shape of a woman. In hindsight, my ex-wife seemed ready-made and waiting with her eastern philosophy, herbal teas and lasagna. The *I Ching* and some hot sake sealed my fate. Shortly afterwards, when I tied myself to a two-year lease and an office job, and as the bathroom filled with bottles and tubes, sprays and lotions, her robe and underwear hanging on the back of the door next to mine, I realized that we'd misinterpreted the ancient book of change. It was already too late.

A Death Toll of One

"Marvin," she said, as I let myself through the door and picked up the receiver. "Please don't say a word. Just let me talk."

I waited.

"You know how I feel. I need to…"

Just then the ground under me shook.

"Did you feel that?" I asked. I heard an alarm on her end, someone screaming in the background. I replaced the phone on the hook and went into the kitchen and put on a pot of coffee.

"I dreamed someone was trying to push me over a cliff," Marie said, walking into the kitchen, rubbing her eyes.

"Is that what woke you up?"

"Yeah, the edge of the cliff was crumbling away under my feet."

"There was an earthquake," I told her.

"A big one?"

"It was like the first time I had sex. Everything shook around for a few seconds then it was all over before I realized what had happened."

She laughed. "It's just as well, I have to get up anyway."

"Coffee?"

"Yeah, I have to go in for training in a couple of hours. I didn't tell you, I found a job."

I waited for her to go on.

"It's no big deal. An entry level position at the FotoStop on Polk Street."

I poured her coffee, hesitant to say anything, hoping this would be a step towards independence for both of us.

"At least I'll be able to chip in with the bills and stuff," she said.

"Don't worry about it, you don't have to."

She nodded and took one of the Stella D'oro biscuits from its package. I couldn't help but watch as she dunked the biscuit into her coffee. Despite the absurdity of the situation and my better intentions, I realized I was beginning to have feelings for her—feelings that weren't exactly clear. What I had to admit though, was that I genuinely liked, and even more so, admired her. She seemed to possess all the straight-talking, clear-thinking qualities I lacked.

She looked up. "Something wrong?"

"Nothing," I said, and she squinted but didn't say anything. When she was done, she got up, put her cup in the sink and then walked over and planted a kiss on my forehead.

A report on the radio estimated the quake damage at over ten million dollars and put the death toll, a housepainter who fell from a ladder while trimming out a Victorian's third-story window, at one.

Somewhere in the building a baritone belted out Ha Più Forte Sapore, from Puccini's *Tosca*. I heard the shower go on and walked over to my desk to begin the translation but with sunlight streaming through the windows and Scarpia's operatic gloating, decided to put work aside and seek out my own version of hidden beauty, truth and meaning, an alternative to Tosca's death in song.

Rummaging through the hall closet I put my kit together and headed for the station. A streetcar dropped me close to one of my favorite groves about halfway through the park. I sat in a small clearing and listened to the birds as I searched among the greenery. Several specimens floated through the air around me. When I spied the perfect creature alight on a leaf of miner's lettuce, I got to my feet.

"Hey, what do you think you're doing?" a burly man with a beard and a Grateful Dead shirt asked me as I reached into my net for the Swallowtail.

I didn't know how to answer, as what I was doing seemed obvious.

His companion, a tall, skinny girl with straight blonde hair that hung past her shoulders looked at me with disdain.

"Let it go," the man said, sounding angry and walking up to me as if to make himself more threatening.

"Who are you?" I asked.

Without saying anything he grabbed my net and bent the handle around his knee. His abrupt action jarred me and without realizing it I had ripped a wing off the butterfly. We all stood there and watched for a second as it lay on the ground wounded, desperately fluttering. A horrible sight. Then I picked up the net and swung the straight half of the handle hitting him across the side of the head.

"You little motherfucker," he said, bringing his hand up to his face. The girl stood there frozen. I brought my foot down on the struggling insect and when the man took a step towards me, I hit him again, across the other side of his face.

"Fuck," he said, now holding his face in his hands, crouching down.

I threw the remains of the broken net at his feet and walked away.

"Asshole!" the girl screamed after me.

When I got home Marie was gone and the phone was ringing. I pulled the shades. For no apparent reason I thought of the fallen housepainter. I wondered what color he had been using.

I was back in my castle. It was time for libation.

Weddings and Dungeons

The job entailed operating a register and feeding film through a processing machine, then packing the prints that came out the other end into an envelope. Marie's workmates were mostly her own age but certainly not like friends from her own neighborhood. Almost the entire staff was gay and lesbian kids, escapees from their parents' homes in far off towns.

They were nice enough though, and when the manager stepped out for a while after her training session, they made a genuine effort to make Marie feel welcome. One of the boys, Darren, came over and let her in on the secret of the FotoStop's success: a reputation for printing anything and everything brought in by head-hanging, middle-aged men who took snaps that sometimes fell to the far side of the law.

"What they do is their business, the manager will tell you, if you bring it up," Darren said, then continued in imitation of their boss, "we're here to do business, not judge."

"Check this out," he signaled to the back of the shop. "Some of our regulars." He flipped through a stack of envelopes and picked out a few, pulling photos from them and narrating: "Man with Dog comes in about once every two weeks. And this is Closet Wife. Here we have Dick and Jane and Dick and Jane… anyway you get the idea."

Marie nodded, a nervous grin across her face.

"Believe it or not, you get used to it… usually. Although there are some things…"

"Like what?"

"Well, there's this one budding Mapplethorpe," Darren said, "pretty normal-seeming, except he has this uncanny knack of getting to highway collisions before the ambulance does. They're not so pretty. Basically though, the biggest challenge is keeping the wedding and graduation pictures apart from the dungeon ones."

Rescued Tumbler, Smiling Duck

Gregorian chants from a neighbor's apartment echoed through the building. I mixed another drink and filled the tub. Despite the incident at the park I was filled with happiness. Sayama would be with me at dawn. Tosca was dead. Marie was gone.

I had attained a certain equilibrium sinking into the bath, drink in hand, that so often eluded me. The only challenge now was to pace myself, and be fresh for our engagement. Maybe take a nap and treat myself to a good meal.

I placed the smiling yellow rubber-duck soap holder into the bath with me and watched it float along with a cake of soap on its back.

Water was something the Japanese understood, the pleasures of a hot bath. In fact, when I was with Sayama we often set ourselves near a body of water: pounding surf or tranquil pond.

It began to rain and I listened to raindrops pinging off the little window high up on the wall above the tub. I poured out another few fingers and squeezed the rubber duck. Ecstatic.

There was a story I used from *True Tales From The News, A Beginning Intermediate ESL Reader*, when I taught in Japan. It showed a picture of a little white dog swimming through the waves. Two couples living on an island each owned a dog. When one couple moved to a neighboring island, the little white dog, lonely for its friend, swam back everyday to visit. It was a famous love story. Someone even made a movie about it.

Completely relaxed for the first time in days, I laid back and absorbed the therapeutic, aquatic environment, as if I were floating. Then suddenly, I was waking up with the phone ringing and the bathwater turned cold. My tumbler of whisky had hit bottom along with the rubber duck. I got out of the bath and searched the medicine cabinet for aspirin. The phone rang again. With a towel around my waist I padded into the living room and answered.

"Marvin," the woman said, "if you won't talk to me I don't know what I'll do."

I hung up. Immediately it rang again. I walked back into the bathroom and drained the tub, rescuing my tumbler and the drowned duck that continued to smile.

Big Money

Marie took up her post inside the park along the cyclone fence. Her brother and sister played on the walk in front of the flat. She checked her watch. Six-thirty. Soon, she told herself. It was all she could do to keep from calling out to them. But that's not what she'd come for. She just wanted to get the times right.

Some boys were playing basketball across from her, no one she recognized. A couple of old men, Puerto Rican or Cuban, sat and gestured on one of the benches not far from her. Then she spotted him, Steve, in a muscle-tee, turning the corner. That was all she wanted. To get his schedule. She got up and walked across the park to the exit at the opposite end, before he even got to the house. She didn't want to chance him seeing her—at least for now.

A few blocks over she turned the corner. A light showed from the third story window. Marie tossed pebbles against one of the panes then undid the chain from the gate of the lot behind the building and mounted the back stairs, two at a time.

"Hurry up," Mariel said when she reached the door. Quickly striding down the hall to Mariel's room, she could almost taste the air. The after-dinner aroma mixed with the warmth of a full house gave off a scent she hadn't realized she missed until that very moment. She could hear the television tuned to the Spanish station in the front room.

Marie passed Mariel's younger sister asleep in the half-light, climbed out the window to the roof of the building next door and waited for her friend. From the doorway to her bedroom Mariel yelled down the hall, "I'm going out on the roof."

"*Por que?*" her grandfather asked, loud enough to be heard above the television.

"To get some air," she answered.

"*Esta bien,*" her grandmother called back. "*No tardes, eh.*"

They made their way across the lower neighboring roof to a ladder that hung off the side of the building, and climbed up, settling themselves into a corner that had always been reserved for just the two of them. With their backs to the retaining wall, they looked out across the city towards the bridge. On their left, the downtown skyline was trimmed in golden edges, while straight ahead lay the low-slung block-long buildings originally used for manufacturing, where rich people now lived under rusting smoke stacks.

Neither of them said a word. Mariel lit two cigarettes and passed one to Marie. "So what…"

"Shh." Marie put her finger to her lips. One of the roving trios that played the corner cantina for tips was belting out a ranchera. She thought of the times her father—wherever he might now be—threw open the window and leaned on the sill to listen. Sometimes he would sing along with them. The music made her want to cry. "I think he went back to Mexico," she said.

"Who? Your father?"

Marie nodded. "I miss him. Even when he was drunk. If he were here none of this would've happened—and that motherfucker would be dead."

"Your mother wants you home," Mariel said. "She thinks we all know where you are, and she told me to tell you nothing would happen if you came back."

"Nothing will happen." Marie flicked her cigarette in a long spiraling arc. "It already did, and she doesn't even believe me. How can she think that I'll ever go back to that house? How could she…"

"What are you going to do? Stay with that guy?"

Marie didn't answer.

"And that gun. The whole thing is starting to scare me. Why don't you stay here? I can talk to my grandmother."

Marie shook her head, no. She turned away, looking out among the hills; she didn't want Mariel to see her face. The trio was still playing. A few tears let loose and rolled down her cheeks. Someone must have been paying them big money.

Schnauzer on the Doorstep

Marie was asleep. I hadn't heard her come in. I glanced over at the alarm clock—less than an hour to go—then went into the kitchen and loaded up the Mr. Coffee coffee machine and went through my morning routine trying not to think about Sayama, which was impossible. As usual, before our meetings, the minutes dragged with no connection to the normal movement of time, as if I were floating in outer space. I caught myself looking up at the clock every few minutes. The wait seemed endless and I became increasingly anxious.

With her the relationship was singular and extraordinary. We relied purely on our projections. As tortured as we pretended to be by the situation there was no denying we relished our rare form of contact that encompassed intellect and imagination. We each knew the unbound person in the other, the one kept hidden. But at the same time she remained a mystery, as I'm sure I was for her, and deep down

I couldn't tell what I was more in love with—Sayama, or the mystery. We teased ourselves with the idea of our physical beings. We intended, one day, to meet, and hold onto one another forever. I shuddered to think of it. Then again, it was a moment that probably would never come.

As usual she appeared at the appointed time and there I was, waiting. The encounter began with warm sake and red satin. We reclined in a Kyoto garden under a yellow slipper of a moon and marveled at the wonder of it all, while fish streaked in luminous silver motion across the obscure waters of a pond. Sayama and I made love on the steps of a gazebo.

We parted with tender promises; she scurried off into the darkness and disappeared in a thicket of bamboo—in reality she was leaving her office to take the subway home.

I felt renewed, and after a quick shower walked into the bedroom to discover Marie was already gone. For a moment I became unglued. Where could she have gone so early? Her job?

I probably should have stayed home and worked on the translation but I wanted time to think, and there was no better place for that than Union Square—the concrete wall held my thoughts better than anywhere else. When I struck my thinking pose and people looked up at "a man thinking," I was aware for once of what I was doing. Not that thinking would be impossible elsewhere, but at home or in the donut shop, library, or bar I tended towards drifting. This type of concentrated, gilded musing had become a refuge.

Even though I was mostly alone with my thoughts, I was hardly ever being alone with my thoughts, which is not the same thing. And that's not to say that I thought of myself as a thinker, I was just thinking, and while I was, I picked up the phone and dialed.

"Yup," he answered, as he often did.

"I'm castling."

"Uh-huh," he replied, then hung up.

When I walked out my front door the schnauzer was waiting. How he found out where I lived I had no idea. It's nerve-wracking enough to have someone follow you but when the dog fell in behind me I couldn't help but think that I'd somehow slipped down the food chain a couple of notches. I couldn't imagine what he wanted, and anytime I turned around to try to find out, he stopped in his tracks and gave me that head-tilting canine-type query I had no clue how to decipher. I don't even like dogs.

That Much Closer

Marie watched as the truck pulled out of the warehouse at 9:30. She got up off the stoop as it turned onto Fourteenth, and again on Folsom, then she returned to the warehouse. A man stood by a line of delivery vans with a clipboard, observing, as one of the vehicles was being loaded.

"Hey," she called to him. "Do you know if Steve's already gone?"

The man looked up from his work.

"He forgot his wallet," she said. "I thought I could catch up with him."

"You have a car?" the man asked.

"Yeah."

He flipped through some pages. "945 Folsom and 863 Howard are his first two stops," he told her.

"Thanks," she said, and walked back out the door. Now she knew three places she could find him on a Tuesday morning.

Afterward, she took a window seat at a corner café and knocked on the window when she saw Mariel. "How's school?" she asked as Mariel pranced in, smiling.

"What are you doing in the neighborhood? You decided to come back?"

"I found a job."

"If you want to sleep over, meet me after school," Mariel said.

Marie nodded and studied the street. A smile spread, suddenly, across her face. She rapped against the glass with a knife handle. The door swung open and Ricardo walked in. "You run away and don't tell me nothing," he said, squinting at her with that face he always wore when he was annoyed with her.

"See you later, Marie," Mariel told her, picking up her books. "And remember what I said."

"Give me a break, Ricardo."

"Give you a break. What happened, that asshole beat you? You want I should do something?"

She shook her head, no, and made a face.

"I should beat your ass," he said, in a way she knew meant he had missed her. "You be around?"

"Later on, if you want me to."

"Yo! I make time for you."

"Okay." She smiled.

"Why don't you pass by, maybe around ten or eleven. I'll be watching from the window."

She knew he was asking her to stay over. He would sneak her into his house.

"Okay?"

She smiled.

"One more absence and they suspend me, then my pop suspend me from a light pole. I'm outta here." He kissed her on the cheek and made for the door, then turned towards her again. "I be waiting for you."

She watched him make his way up the street and decided it was time to leave. While waiting for the bus, she debated whether to take Mariel up on the offer—it would put her that much closer to Steve.

Man on Fire

The schnauzer followed me all the way to the Square. When I struck my pose he sat, a few feet off, and didn't move. With two or three fingers of gold metallic paint he could have easily been part of the act. Occasionally a child would try to lure him into play, or someone would lean over and pat his head, but he wouldn't allow himself to be distracted. And though he maintained a stiff pose, I noticed his eyes moving back and forth in search of something.

It was obvious that the dog had had a place once, and was now either lost or abandoned. In some ways the little four-legger reminded me of my mother, a truly tragic figure whose life had somehow come unanchored and was now adrift. But her dilemma, unlike the schnauzer's, had a complexity about it somewhat more abstract. One in which I felt myself, as an unwilling player, primarily responsible.

Tragedy, by its very nature, is a complicated convolution. I remembered reading a philosopher who defined it, roughly, as when two principled individuals, both justified and rational in regards to the truth of their beliefs, and of unshakeable resolve, meet head on. Quite simply, no one is wrong, only the two rights are opposed to one another, each person unwilling to give in. With my brother as the lightning rod, my mother and I stood at opposite poles. Furthermore, I had my own guilt at not being able to comfort her.

A pair of kids, fresh from school, aiming spitballs at me, soon roused me from my intrafamilial reverie. They were trying for my eyes. The schnauzer tensed. "Let's get some pebbles," one of them said. The few people watching held their ground, apparently taking a perverse interest in the unfolding scene. They were tourists, which allowed them to relinquish responsibility. No matter what the social dynamics in a given situation, they felt they had the right to stand off to the side and casually observe an event, no matter how gruesome. Some of them even took pictures.

One of the small, solid projectiles rocketed off my head. A group of northern Europeans became excited and chattered among themselves—probably something about cruelty in America. Another hard object hit me in the neck. Then another bounced off my forehead. The Europeans dropped a few coins in my hat and hurried away. "This motherfucker don't move," one of the boys said. "Let's make a fire," the other one suggested. "I bet that make him budge."

One of the disadvantages of my stance was that even though I had a near one hundred-eighty degree horizontal view, if needed, I could not see straight down to my feet—unless I moved my head. And that's exactly where the boy had positioned himself. The schnauzer tilted his head, and I was trying to read from his expression whether the boy was about to set my trouser cuffs aflame. The gold metallic coating, being highly flammable, especially worried me.

I thought I could feel heat, though not very much, and I wasn't sure if it was my imagination or not. The schnauzer gave no sign of anything unusual. The boy at my feet screamed and the other one backed away. Two little kids with Styrofoam bats, the same ones from a few days earlier, came from behind me and into my field of view. Behind them was the woman I'd given the cigarette to, Jeanette, pulling the boy holding a disposable lighter by his hair away from me. "Get you hands off me," the boy yelled at her.

"You were trying to set that man on fire!" she hollered.

"You don't touch me, bitch."

"Don't touch you! I should smash your fucking face."

A crowd gathered around, but no one was dropping coins into the hat.

"Keep you hands off me, bitch," the boy reiterated as his friend looked on from a safe distance.

"Learn to keep your hands off of other people," she replied, and gave him a shove in the direction of his friend.

"I find out where you live, bitch," the boy said walking away.

Jeanette turned around, ignoring him and came right up to me. "Are you okay, mister?"

She didn't recognize me, and I didn't move. She stood there for a few moments and stared, questioningly, into my eyes. It was the most uncomfortable I had ever been working the Square. Out of nowhere one of the little boys lifted his Styrofoam bat and hit the schnauzer. Jeanette spun around and began to scold him. The schnauzer ran off and Jeanette confiscated both bats, hauling the little boys by their wrists to their common fate.

The Wrong Answer

She had stored the small pack with her belongings under the counter, at her feet. Although the job wasn't interesting, she loved the banter. Her coworkers talked about a thousand things that had never occurred to her or anyone else she knew. It seemed like they had no fear. They would converse on any subject, and argue, just for the sake of it. It made her think about the "toughness" of the people she'd grown up with, and of how afraid, or unprepared they were to expose themselves in conversation by taking a stand. Best of all, these people at her job included her. Asked what she thought, and how she felt about things.

During the afternoon, they had her work with the processor. Again, she was with Darren and they joked and laughed about some of the photos. Transgender weddings. Women bound in Saran Wrap. Men in collars and leashes. And of course there were a few images that they had trouble looking at, at all. Inevitably, they would call these to each other's attention, and no matter how repulsive, some inexplicable curiosity made them look. There was one exception though. A couple of pictures mixed in with a seemingly ordinary batch that took her aback. She dropped the two photos to the floor and said nothing to Darren, packing the remainder into the corresponding envelope. Then, without even thinking, she copied the information—name, address and phone number— from the envelope, and later retrieved the two photos off the floor and stuffed them into her pocket.

When her shift ended, Marie headed back into her neighborhood and positioned herself at the playground on the corner. She recognized some of the faces on the courts, and the players acknowledged her with a nod.

Steve appeared at the anticipated hour and Marie, testing her resolve, reached into her pack and fingered the revolver. She had control, and it was only a matter of letting him know the equation had been inverted. She wanted him to experience the same slow, deliberate horror that she had. Then letting go of the gun, she reached further into her pack and pulled out the two photos. That's when all her thoughts and careful planning were replaced by a wave of fear.

• • •

Mariel already had her head out the window. "I thought you'd come," she said. "Meet me at the back door."

Once up on the roof, while they passed a joint, Mariel began to quiz her. "So where to now?"

"Ricardo told me to come by. I'll probably stay there."

"And after that?"

"I don't know. I'll have to think about it."

"You know you can't just keep floating around," Mariel said.

Marie didn't answer. Instead she stood up and peered from the edge of the roof looking down over the streets she had known her entire life that now seemed altogether different. The neighborhood that had once felt as if it belonged to her seemed to have transformed itself, like she'd never been a part of it. "That's not what's important now," she said, finally.

"If you asked me," Mariel volunteered, "I would think where I was going to sleep at night was pretty damn important."

"I know you would," Marie said, handing her back the joint and lighting a cigarette.

They sat back down. "Marie," Mariel told her, "I'm only trying to help. I'm…"

"I know, I know," Marie cut her off.

The fog began to roll in. Mariel brought her dinner and a blanket. She kept Marie company while doing homework. When it got too cold they came inside and spent almost an hour in Mariel's room. At ten o'clock Marie said her goodbyes and walked the three blocks to Ricardo's.

She could smell the alcohol on his breath but said nothing. Down the hall someone was watching TV. Ricardo undid the drawstring on his sweats and let them drop. He came over to the small bed, where Marie was sitting, and straddled her. What she really wanted was to talk, but that, she realized, was not on the agenda. Ricardo reached down, unsnapped her pants and pulled down the zipper. She didn't resist. Her mind drifted and it seemed that now Ricardo was part of that place she had looked down into from Mariel's roof.

"They told me you was staying with some faggot," Ricardo sneered as he lay next to her, pulling on his cigarette in the dark.

She watched him for a while. His face lit up and his chest glowed red. "He's not," she answered.

"What, queer?" he asked, blowing out smoke, and she realized she should have never come. "You like him?"

She kept silent. Any answer she could give would be the wrong one.

"He fuck you?"

Marie started to cry. She couldn't help it.

"You like it?"

Tibet

Drink in hand, I calmed myself in the emptiness, behind the locked door of my apartment. I wondered where the schnauzer might have gone, and why. What was the point of him going anywhere? Marie still wasn't home. I would have welcomed her company, shaken as I was. The wall I built in my mind when I performed in the Square had been knocked flat. The island of serenity, my inner chamber of contemplation in the midst of all the chaos, had been violated. I wasn't sure if I'd be able to return.

I topped off my whiskey, walked over to my desk and dug into the translation at hand—fractals. The perfection of form found within rupture. I ignored the ringing phone. A theory of geometric precision applied to both natural and inorganic material. Sirens screamed past my window, there was no escape from the wondrous exactitude of our world, and the universe.

I contemplated the labor itself—translation—its literal meaning today, from the Latin, "to carry through," though I preferred to think about the archaic and theological definition, "to convey to heaven without natural death." In that definition, deliverance was implied. I imagined myself as a messenger of clarity able to strip back the masquerade of human tongues to reveal the power behind the words. That which was eternal in itself—meaning. The passing of terminology from one language to another allowed me to turn the words around, symbols became objects. Transference from one culture to the next: the tones, shades and interpretations ultimately transformed, revealing language more as a means of the transport of ideas than the ideas themselves. But in that middle realm, in the decision about whether to use *wondrous, magnificent, splendid, fantastic, superb, brilliant* or *outstanding*, it's possible to understand the load and charge of what is simply uttered. We are truly god-like, it is only the physical world that detains us. Words. Pen and paper. Signs. Symbols. All bound by our explanations.

As the text addressed the splintering fragments of the physical world, I was ready to put it to rest for the night. I had put in more than eight hours and it was past two o'clock in the morning. Marie still hadn't come home. But it wasn't until I pulled back the covers to climb into bed that I noticed her things were gone. I searched the room, and the apartment, for some trace of her.

In that moment, when what I had hoped for since her arrival—her departure—had been realized, I understood that I wanted her there with me, that I craved her presence and the quirky, utterly human interaction between us. The silence echoed around me. Not only did I miss her, I was worried about her. She'd obviously installed herself in my apartment out of desperation, though its origins remained a mystery. In our short time together it had become apparent that Marie wasn't afraid of confrontation. I was fairly certain that her thick-skinned head-down approach to the center of conflict had been compromised—but by what, I couldn't guess, although I was sure that I'd offered a strange sort of stability and protection, a neutral space where she could live without fear.

I tossed around in my bed until sleep came black and thick. It must have taken several minutes before the insistent ringing penetrated my dense Freudian jungle. The day had already dawned and as always I was surprised by my hard-on. My mouth was parched and I needed to pee, I could hardly speak.

"Hello?"

"Marie, is that you?"

"I'm on the corner, buzz me in."

She walked past me, down the hall, to the bedroom and immediately collapsed on the bed. I followed her into the darkened room, covered her, and brushed her hair back from her eyes. In the living room I poured myself a drink and sat on the edge of the coffee table admitting to myself, for the first time, something about my feelings for Marie.

The desperate couplings had relaxed into a warm presence and it occurred to me that someone had filled in the invisible space between me and something nameless. In a crazy way she'd stepped into the shoes of the girl who ran off with my brother. Then I crawled back into bed and curled spoon-like around the fetal Marie.

I slipped into a dream with Sayama in a department store; when I looked up she was gone. Frantic, I searched for her. Then I woke with a start. Marie hadn't moved. I lifted myself up and looked down on the sleeping Marie, content with her presence beside me. What I saw made my stomach twist and twitch. Both her eyes were blackened and one side of her face was swollen yellow to dull black with purple edges. She hugged the pillow to her chest, sleeping sound, deep and peaceful, while I headed for the bathroom to retch.

When she awoke I had coffee and a half-dozen donuts arranged on a plate.

"Hi," she greeted me blearily, shaking a cigarette loose from a pack. I poured coffee into the HEY WAKE UP! Walgreens mug. She sat down, closed her eyes and sipped slowly, carefully, between swollen lips.

I thought of the times I had passed battered women in the supermarket. The acknowledgment written literally on their faces said something truly terrible about all of us. They carried the other end of creation in the battered pulp as a reminder of our awesome nature and fury, our detachment and contradictions.

"Jean Arp once said, 'the law of chance embraces all laws and is unfathomable.' "

She raised her eyebrows, looking up without lifting her head.

"It's the cause, he said, from which all life arises."

She slowly straightened herself up in her chair. "Did you miss me?"

I smiled and handed her half a jelly donut.

When the phone rang Marie picked it up and said, "No, Marvin went to Tibet and won't be back until April. I'll take a message."

The Taste of Anchovies

Of course I wanted to ask her what had happened; she didn't volunteer anything. I felt guilty but wasn't sure why. What I did know was that I felt powerless and inadequate when she needed me most. Everything else at the moment seemed unimportant.

"Do you want to go out somewhere?" she asked, and I jumped at the opportunity.

We both dressed and Marie, I noticed, carefully applied makeup where she could to cover her wounds. I didn't say anything but the makeup only highlighted her bruises.

The schnauzer, sleeping across the front steps, lifted his head as we came out of the building. He let out a meek little bark. Marie crouched down and called him over. I stood a few feet behind Marie and the dog, keeping a cautious eye on me, slowly approached her. She patted him and scratched the scruff of his neck. The schnauzer was in ecstasy.

"Whose dog is it?" Marie asked.

"He doesn't belong to anyone. He lives on the street."

"Doesn't seem like a street dog."

"I know."

Marie kept turning her neck to make sure he was still following us. At the corner she went into the grocery and bought chicken salad from the deli case. "I feel bad leaving him here," she said, putting down the food.

"Don't worry," I told her, "nothing will happen to him. He'll probably still be here when we get back."

Then I took Marie by the hand and we continued down the hill, through the Tenderloin, towards downtown and the museum. There, I thought, our vision of the world and what we wrought from it could somehow again be affirmed, in spite of what had happened. That much, at least, I planned to do for her.

In front of Joseph Stella's bridge, Marie, without taking her eyes off the painting, said, "I think I'm falling in love with you all over again." Something caught in my throat. This was different than before. I wasn't afraid of her words any longer. The shape of our relationship had moved on from frantic, sometimes desperate possession, to something else: a kind of assuredness, however unsteady, in each other.

I felt timid and helpless at her side. We walked arm in arm through the Japanese photography exhibit, and proudly, we stood apart as a piece of hyperrealism wandering through the rooms. The beaten girl at my side assumed an objectified presence in which a primal code had been locked away. We might have been the institution's biggest attraction that afternoon.

Marie was strong and beautiful, sitting there in the courtyard, drinking from a disposable cup. Afterwards we went to see a Hong Kong kung fu western. The night was warm and the shops and restaurants and bars left their doors open. After the movie we wound through North Beach trying on hats and sunglasses and buying postcards and herbal cigarettes to smoke with our cappuccinos at a corner café.

The crudely rolled thin brown cylinder hung from her fat lip as she looked side to side at the remnants of desolation's angels talking into their beards. The woman at the next table read the tarot for a man with a hook instead of a right hand. Someone was playing an accordion out on the street.

"I think now I'm happy," she said.

"Why do you say that?"

She grabbed my hand and smiled. "Because."

Once home we called for pizza and sat in front of the television without watching it. I waited for her to tell me what had happened but instead she chattered on about the Giant's recent three-player trade. I wanted her to tell me something. To make it all better for the both of us.

"So what about the butterflies?" she suddenly asked.

And with that I poured two tumblers of single malt I'd been saving for a special occasion, and took her on a voyage through the past, over the trails and back roads of Asia, South America and Africa. She quizzed me carefully and brought to the fore what I had purposely pushed as far back as I could. When she finally wound her way back to my brother, I was crying on the couch. She wrapped herself around me tenderly, and all I could think of was the girl who had left me for him. The next thing I knew I was waking up on my bed with her snoring softly at my side.

It was almost six before I pulled myself from bed and managed to get to my computer with a cup of coffee. Sayama was already there, waiting patiently.

"I have something important to tell you," she began. But first she hedged and teased with the preliminary mundane facts of life that we shared: Her husband's temper. Her boss's ongoing affairs with newer secretaries. A recent purchase. Dinner. The stuff that holds our day-to-day lives together. That was our ritual, even though we knew that what we wanted from one another was quite the opposite.

After her initial banter, while I was trying to keep down last night's pizza, she finally came out with it. "I'm coming!" she exclaimed. "They're going to have some kind of meeting with the Hermanos Jimenez in Los Angeles, and want to bring their own interpreter."

I was happy and confused—shocked.

"There's one catch though."

"What?" I asked hesitantly.

"My husband is coming with me."

By the time we had bidden each other farewell, Sayama had spelled out the entire plan. It would lead to her liberation, her husband's humiliation, and ultimately bring us together. It was something I had always dreamed of but never imagined possible.

My head was pounding by the time I lifted myself out of the chair and walked away from my desk. I crawled back into bed and pulled the covers over my head. Marie turned over and moaned. I put my arm around her. Pizza rumbled somewhere deep inside my intestines. My burp tasted of anchovies and I fell back asleep in a salted, gustatory ambience that reminded me of dockside eateries.

Tea and Scones

It must have been afternoon when I opened my eyes, Maria Callas was belting out Bellini's *La Sonnambula*, in a register, and at a decibel level, which at first made me think someone was screaming. I called out and no one answered. Marie was gone. Panicked, I pulled myself from bed and went to look for her and found a note on the kitchen table saying she was at work and would be back. I couldn't imagine her wanting to go to work after what had happened.

Coffee was already made and I added a taste of bourbon. I turned on the radio then noticed the "Missing" flier taped to the refrigerator with Marie's face. She was smiling. I had seen her smile before—plenty of times—but this was different, an innocence that would never again be recovered. It reminded me of the photograph my mother had on her wall of my brother and me, arms around one another. A Christmas when we still believed Santa Claus came down the chimney without even having one. Whenever I saw myself on her wall and looked into my eyes, I didn't recognize the child staring back.

After my second cup, I cut out the coffee altogether. A doctor on the radio talked about teenage suicides and took phone calls from the public. She spoke about the warning signs: according to her, if I were a teenager, alarms would be wearing down their armature casings to get me help.

I wondered if fractal theorists could locate the unity in a teenager with his head in an oven. For some reason my neighbor abruptly switched from opera to ambient sounds, primates calling to one another. The phone rang and I thought it might be Marie.

I must have slurred my greeting, because my mother asked, "Is that Dean Martin?"

"That's *amore*," I said.

"You sound drunk."

"I worked through the night."

"Did you even eat breakfast?"

"I had an olive."

"I just called to see how you were."

"Smashing. And you, mother dear?"

"I'm old and worried that my son will never work a real job, get married or have children. Other than that I'm fine."

"That's good to hear. How's the weather?"

"I'm in Florida, how do you think the weather is? Besides, I'm the one who's supposed to ask the weather questions."

"Sunny and cool."

"I didn't ask you about the weather. What I *am* curious about is the girl who picked up the phone the last time I called."

"A girl answered the phone?"

"Not unless you've been hanging around with the castrati."

"Oh, you mean Marie. She's just a friend staying here for awhile."

"She sounded a little young."

"She's young at heart, just like you."

"You better take it easy with the booze, buster. Did you know tomorrow is your brother's birthday?"

"Yes, I did," I lied.

"I just thought you should know."

"I do."

"Thirty-seven."

I didn't say anything. Her television was on. I could picture her sitting all the way to one side of the couch. Frowning at the screen.

"Take care of yourself, son," she said.

After hanging up I poured the remaining bourbon from my cup down the drain. My head was too clouded to continue the translation as I should have. All over America teenagers were committing suicide. My mother sat in her air-conditioned living room watching game shows. Primates chattered. I had to make some changes before Sayama arrived. I turned off the radio and opened the hall closet.

A few minutes later I was tapping down the street with my white cane and impenetrable sunglasses. People got out of my way. As a blind man, I walked the hills to a dancer's rhythm unstringing the knots balled up inside of me. At the center of the bind was Marie. I found myself daydreaming of something real and permanent—and it could never happen. She was a very young woman with a life ahead of her and I was anchored by the deadweight of age. Even though she offered herself I couldn't allow it, although I had to admit I wanted it, more than anything—even more than Sayama.

"Are you alright?" an elderly woman with a shopping bag stared up at me and asked. It wasn't until that moment I realized tears were streaming down my cheeks.

"I'm okay. Thanks."

"Pardon me for sticking my nose where it doesn't belong," she said, "but it doesn't seem so at all."

"It's good to cry," I answered.

"Yes, it is," she said, looking hard into my face, scrutinizing. "I was just going to get a spot of tea in the shop across the road. Would you care to join me?"

"You're very kind but no, thanks."

"I should enjoy the company very much," she insisted. "An old woman like me hasn't very many people left to talk to."

As I stood there, indecisive, she grabbed my arm and guided me across the street. Without even asking she ordered me a cup of ginger tea and a scone. "Sometimes all you need," she said, "is a strong cup of tea and someone to talk to. Strangers are the best because you can get it off your chest without the threat of it coming back to you at an inopportune moment—after all, you'll probably never see the person again."

Two cups of tea and scones were placed before us. I still hadn't said a word before she spoke up once more. "So why all the sadness, young man?"

"It's a girl," I confessed.

She raised her brow and I had to look down at the table not to give myself away with a sudden change of expression. I caught her watching me as I felt around for my scone. "This girl," I continued, "is quite a bit younger than me and I like her very much."

She smiled.

"The problem is that she's so young I don't think it would work out."

"Maybe she knows what's in store for her and has accepted it. After all she could be a great help to you."

"I've thought of that. The situation is she came to me for shelter, she's in some kind of trouble at home—she still lives with her family. To me it's obvious that what I offer is both security and freedom. You see, it's an age thing, something she'll find on her own soon, although she doesn't quite realize it yet. It wouldn't be fair to her."

The old woman didn't answer right away. Instead she sat there sipping her tea.

"Though the truth is," I added, "I care for her very much."

"You are a very courageous man," she said, putting down her cup. "And noble, I might add. The things we love are the most difficult to give up, even though we must."

I nodded in agreement, and our conversation continued on an alternative track. The woman knew when enough was enough; she insisted on paying and we parted with a handshake at the door. I watched her walk slowly down the street with her shopping bag and already missed her company.

The Streets of My Imagination

With the last light of the sun, banks of fog began to drift through the valley. I approached my building, damp and shivering. Marie still hadn't arrived. I changed my clothes and settled in at my desk, interrupted by the phone.

"Marvin, if you would only listen to me for a minute," she started.

I hung up immediately.

Fractals ate up the clock as I struggled with the symmetry of the universe and the ringing phone, wanting to pick it up if it were Marie but convinced it would be another plea for Marvin. The disrupted rhythm made it impossible to continue, and after a few hours I decided to take a break.

Marie came through the door as I was laying out my black jacket and clerical collar. She gave me a big, lopsided smile, and asked, "Mind if I come along?"

I was relieved to see her. "Grab a sweater," I said.

There was a steady drizzle as we climbed the hill. Marie handed me an envelope stuffed with photos. "Duplicates," she said.

"Thanks" I told her, "I can't wait to have a look," before stuffing them into my pocket. She explained the nature of the operation and readied me for what I might find.

"Like I said, I'm looking forward to it. Besides, now you've made me curious. You could probably buy better stuff in the magazine and video stores on Polk Street."

"I don't think that's the same," she snapped.

Although vague, her words, an angry challenge, resonated and made me understand something about her I didn't have the courage to address, so instead I shrugged my shoulders. The truth was, she probably knew better than I did.

As we walked into the bar, my eyes adjusted to the light and I was met by a wide grin. It was the pierced redhead clinging to a barstool, the same one, in fact.

"Father," she called out, "c'mon and have a drink."

I walked over with Marie and introduced them. The redhead looked her over, whistled, and asked, "What happened, honey?"

Marie looked down and mumbled, "Nothing."

The redhead put her arm around Marie, and said, "It's okay. I know exactly how you're feeling, believe me." Then she turned to me and asked, "So what brought you in, Father, the rain?"

The evening turned into something of a social gathering when the bartender came over and exclaimed, "It's you!

You'll never believe what happened with that address you gave me!"

I suggested we move over to a table so as not to have to hear about it, but after putting down the drinks the bartender pulled up a chair. "It was like she'd been waiting for me. It was the strangest thing, I rang the doorbell and walked right in."

I felt my face go flush.

"So you and the good Father are friends?" the redhead asked Marie.

"More than that."

The woman looked at me sharply. "You're not a nun?" she asked.

Marie laughed. "Only if he wants me to be."

I was beginning to feel a bit uncomfortable.

"Let me get this round," the bartender chimed in to break the silence that followed. "A nun," he chuckled. "She told me her ex-husband would have her dress up as all kinds of weird shit," he said before going off to pour the drinks.

Marie looked at me and smiled as the redhead played with her long silky hair. Outside the drizzle turned to rain. The redhead rolled a cigarette from a pouch of Dutch tobacco and passed it back and forth between Marie and herself.

There was no end to the bartender's ex-husband stories.

"I'd like to meet that guy," the redhead said while Marie collapsed giggling into her lap.

The drinks came free, fast and frequently, and I took full advantage. The night, in fact, became a blur—not even—the memory of a blur. In the morning, without knowing how it happened, I found the redhead on my couch when I got up to keep my appointment with Sayama.

I put on the coffee and looked over at her sleeping that alcoholic sleep, black and tight around her very being. It reminded me of those mornings where even the light from opening my eyes gave me a headache. I'm sure she didn't remember how she got to where she was either. Then I looked around in a sudden panic, relieved at not finding the bartender asleep in a corner.

As I switched on the machine my chest tightened with excitement and fear. I don't know why, but at that moment I decided to click on her name and see her photo. My heart was in my mouth as the picture formed. There she was, at the edge of a bed looking up at the photographer with a sad sort of smile on her face. I was surprised by her innocent beauty, her long, thin face with its certain softness around the lips. Just looking at the picture I knew she had told me more about how she felt and what she thought than she had ever told anyone else. You could tell she was timid in social situations, awkward, always trying hard to make a good impression but not much for words. Looking at her you'd guess that she could never have said the things she had to me, aloud.

"Are you afraid?" Sayama asked.

"Yes. Are you?"

"Of course I am."

We anticipated the unknown, the flipside of ourselves. The people we were to everyone else. Sayama said it felt like we were moving back together, through a mirror where we'd been living, vicariously, for so long. In an uncertain way we were already in mourning.

"Shouldn't we be making plans?" I asked.

"You mean for when I get there?"

"For always."

"Yeah, I guess so, I don't know. Where do we begin?"

Before, Sayama obliterated the past and present. When I had a job and a wife and a brother, all Sayama would have needed to do was step through the door for everything to change. That would have been plenty. It was the only plan we really ever had, at least in our imaginations. But now, the ethereal realm of Sayama was a little sticky around the edges.

"There's a lot I need to tell you," I said.

"Me too."

"Then maybe we should just wait until…"

"Good idea."

We had always believed that nothing else could matter outside ourselves. I thought having Sayama in my life would somehow cast a shadow so large as to make all the mistakes, fears, regrets and failures up till then insignificant. She fearlessly inhabited the jeweled streets of my imagination. She was the one I'd been hungering for and now I was full of apprehension.

Saying Her Name

I passed the redhead, now sprawled across the couch, face up, with one arm dramatically posed across her forehead. Marie was already at the kitchen table, smoking, as if she had been waiting for me. I wondered how I could explain Sayama's imminent arrival, which words I would use. I worried. What could I say? I poured some coffee and sat down across from her.

"Hi," she said.

She looked pitiful. The hurt turned ugly. What I had seen in her at the museum, a vivacious and brilliant courage, was an illusion, a lie. She was a girl cowering behind tough talk and swagger.

"A real bender last night," I said.

She twisted a piece of hair in her fingers, pulled on her cigarette.

"Do you want something to eat? Some eggs?" I asked.

"Sure."

I turned to her after I had gotten up and looked into the refrigerator blankly. I became stuck in the moment. Frozen. The way her right eyelid puffed out crimson and purple. The healing split lip. I walked over to where she was sitting and crouched down in front of her, taking her hands in mine, and asked her, "Marie, who did this?"

Her eyes dropped, first to her knees, then to the floor, but she didn't loosen her grip.

"I don't know what to say, Marie. I don't know what I should do."

She let go of one of my hands and pulled me closer. I laid my head in her lap. She laughed, let out a small chuckle and I looked up, surprised. She lifted her eyes and shot me a crooked smile. "I had an uncle," she said, "who I guess you could say ran into some bad luck. People were after him. One night, my aunt gets a call saying they found his car parked on the Golden Gate with a suicide note in it. They found his shoes on the bridge but they never found the body."

"Why would anyone take off their shoes first?" I asked.

"I want to be just like him," she said. "Nobody will ever be sure."

There was nothing to say. I hung in the odd space opening around us and waited.

"You know what you can do?" she asked, picking up another thread of the conversation.

"What?"

"Tell me what you see here," she said, sifting through the pile of newspapers and magazines on the chair beside her, pulling out the envelope of photographs she had given me the night before.

Shuffling through the stack of images, she picked one out, a photograph of a very young girl sitting in a chair with her dress pulled up, exposing herself, and laid it down in front of me. The expression on the little girl's face was not all that easily read. I couldn't decide between uncertainty and disdain.

I handed the photo back to her. It was obvious what I saw. I had seen it before, and I didn't need to say it. In fact it was the reverse. Marie was answering my earlier question about what had happened to her, that much became obvious.

She put the whole bunch back in the envelope and looked as if she were waiting for me to ask her something. I lifted my head imploringly in her direction. "So what are you going to do with it?"

"You need to write your name, address and phone number on the envelope," she told me, matter of fact.

I flipped the eggs, once, in the pan and paused before sliding them onto a plate. "And?"

"We can already guess what you would do."

I put the eggs down in front of her. "What's that?"

She looked at me in a way that either said she was hurt or felt sorry for me, though it hardly made a difference. "Nothing," she said in a manner that made it hard to know if that's what she'd thought I'd do, or she wanted to drop the conversation. Then she began to pick at her eggs.

As I searched for a rejoinder the redhead stumbled into the kitchen and saved me from having to say anything. "I could use some of that," she said, waving a hand towards the Mr. Coffee coffee machine while reaching for the pack of cigarettes on the kitchen table.

I left them both in the kitchen and got dressed before quietly letting myself out. I headed for the library, down Larkin Street past the sidewalk sale offering eight-track players, unnecessary kitchen appliances and leftover shoes. As I glanced at the outmoded merchandise, I thought of my mother, whose general complaint with life was that nothing ever seemed to fit quite right. Her sarcasm was her only sense of relief, a stubborn reflex held over from the days before she'd given up. Had she played, she would have been a better chess player than me. She at least had the ability to justify opposition by her attitude—and whether she was right or wrong, winner or loser, you could never step away from any match with her and feel completely clean, thanks to the tenacity born of something unshakable in her.

At the reading table, I stared at a copy of Fear and Trembling. It was difficult to concentrate. Did Marie really plan to make contact with the girl in the photo? The whole chain of recent events—Marie taking refuge with me, the violence, her reaction to the disturbing poses—pretty much clued me in to what Marie feared. But maybe it would be for the best if she found the girl, maybe she could do for the girl what I was unable to do for her. At the least, she would let the girl know she wasn't alone. And, it might be a way for Marie to help herself. Though really, I was out of my league. I couldn't imagine being so completely and utterly violated.

When I returned home they were on the couch with the television on and didn't hear me come in. I made my way, quietly, into the kitchen and picked up the envelope with the photos. In one of them the girl lay across a single bed, more factual than sexual, starkly exhibiting what might be read as disinterest veiling a vague curiosity, or vice-versa. Then there were a few shots of her jogging down the beach with a little brown and white terrier, and snaps of the Cliff House and Seal Rock. In the last image she stood in front of the old Sutro Baths site, against a rail, wearing a pair of yellow shorts and yellow- and white-checked blouse, smiling directly into the camera.

Something caught in my throat. The smiling girl, if I read it right, was trying to obliterate the fear and horror of the reality she lived. In that moment I understood Marie's interest in her as a way to reconcile something in her own situation. Beyond that, the more I looked into that smiling face, the more it became tied to my own sense of self. My world had crashed around me when my ex-girlfriend confessed her liaison with my own flesh and blood, and now he was dead, my mother couldn't bring herself to accept it, and the only one left to confront was me.

"Good to see ya," the redhead called out as I walked into the living room.

"She's been here all day," Marie whispered, getting up to greet me.

I sat down on the couch and poured a drink from the bottle of single malt my guest had been enjoying.

"You got good taste," she said, sipping her drink.

I pried off my shoes and clicked through the channels. Marie laid her head on my shoulder.

"So you never told me what it is that you do," I said, not taking my eyes from the screen.

"Do!" she laughed. "I do just about anything… well, not anymore."

A picture of a woman, from a photograph, flashed across the screen and caught my attention. The newscaster said: "Jeanette Petrovich, 33, of San Francisco's Bay View District, was found dead along with her two sons, Aaron seven, and Mark six, in the garage of 3775 Shoreline Drive, this afternoon by police."

The report hit me with such force that my chest tightened and I went dizzy. It was the woman I had talked to outside Grace Cathedral, the one that had saved me from the two boys at Union Square. I turned up the volume.

"Apparent causes of death," the newscast continued, "are Petrovich's suicide by asphyxiation, in which she took the lives of her two young children, although the case is still under investigation."

I remembered how she told me she could use some luck. I turned the volume back down.

"What was that?" Marie asked.

"Another hard luck story," the redhead growled.

"Someone I knew."

"You knew her?" Marie asked, lifting her head from my shoulder.

I remembered the man in the beat-up car with the hanging fender who came to pick her up. "Yeah," I said.

"Well, you sure get around," the redhead spat out, then began to laugh uncontrollably, which brought on a fit of coughing that doubled her over and sent her stomping out of the room. I almost felt I could cry.

"She passed out before," Marie said.

It took me a moment to comprehend what Marie had said. "I'll be back in a little while," I told her and headed for the door.

On my way up the hill, I stopped at the corner store and bought a pack of Shermans, then proceeded to the Square. I sat on the same bench where we had talked those few minutes and lit a cigarette, looking out to where the two boys had hit each other with their Styrofoam bats while laughing and screaming. The afternoon was postcard perfect, with big billowy clouds skating across the blue. "Jeanette," I said aloud and surprised myself in doing so. The absence sounded in its last silent vowel and came to rest somewhere nameless inside me. I couldn't help but feel I had somehow failed her.

The schnauzer, who had taken up his post under the bench across the path, with his head on his paws, seemed to lift his eyes in lazy agreement.

Back to Nothing

I began by telling Sayama about her. Unconsciously, I think I wanted to lend some weight to a world that up until then had existed only in the imagination, a sort of psychological semiotics the two of us valued for its disembodiment, its purity. I still couldn't imagine a physical presence pertaining to her. I was afraid our mere weight would pull us under the erotic stream of consciousness with mundane details and that the volume of our bodies would cast a heavy and deadly shadow across our virtual luminosity as we entered the world of things together.

That same day the redhead showed up with a "Have You Seen Me" Xerox ripped from a lamppost; it offered a reward. It was also the day Marie went blond.

On top of which Sayama and I had grappled with the transformational nature of our relationship that always seemed to be about communication until we realized it had as much to do with its opposite.

"So where will she go?" Sayama asked finally.

"Don't worry," I assured her, not knowing myself.

When we sat down to coffee, I told Marie straight away about Sayama and our plans. She brushed back the stubby ends of her new closely cropped hair, which did little to disguise her from the image on the refrigerator; her thick lips and high cheekbones were a dead giveaway. "You're asking me to leave," she said, without meeting my gaze.

"Marie," I said, reaching under the table and touching her knee, "this has been a long time coming."

She shook her head, calmly, and said, "Okay," before getting up and retreating to the bedroom.

She had called it right. The more I sat and thought about it the more difficult the situation seemed. She had no place. Given that fact I couldn't help but conjure images of her being further bruised and beaten. She couldn't just leave. Our life, built upon a thin web of uncertainty and speculation, was now, due to her coaxing, a reality that reflected solidity and security that surprised even me.

I grabbed my jacket and walked around the neighborhood aimlessly. Something seemed to snap inside of me. The last few pages of translation and a strike for control of the center of the chessboard hung jittery at the margins of an unsettling present that I unwittingly owned.

Things didn't improve any when I got back to my apartment. A note from Marie on the kitchen table said: "I'm looking for a place. I don't want to stay here tonight. I love you. See you tomorrow." I read it twice.

After two stiff whiskey sodas I dialed my ex-wife's number. It just occurred to me—from nowhere. "Hello," I listened to her familiar voice, then again, "Hello," before hanging up.

Then I dialed my mother, forgetting all about the three-hour difference. She picked up out of a dead sleep.

"Did I wake you?" I asked.

"What's wrong?"

I could hear the trembling in her voice. "Nothing's wrong, I just thought I'd call you. I forgot how late it was there."

You could almost hear all the absences of her life in the three-second silence. "Everything's alright?" she asked.

"Yeah, go back to sleep. I'll call again at a decent hour."

I poured myself another drink. Then I made some coffee. I wondered what had gotten into Joe DiMaggio's head. What was Marilyn going to do with a group of restaurant owners deep-sea fishing in the fog? I looked around, sipping my drink, and realized if Marie was gone all that was left was to tell Sayama, "No." Which would change everything back to nothing. I laughed.

If You Wish to Leave a Message

It was a fight to pick my head up off the kitchen table. The phone had been ringing all morning, and I had been trying to dislodge what felt like an ice pick through my brain that pegged me to the wooden table, and unplug it. At first I only made it as far as the kitchen sink, though I finally succeeded in getting to the bathroom where I spent the better part of the afternoon on the furry blue oval bath mat that all but blotted out the constant telephonic code echoing down the hall.

Later that evening, I heard the click of the lock through the droning CNN commentator and opened my eyes. She waved and I arced my palm over my brow to see her face.

"Guess what?" she asked from across the room.

I pushed a sound out from the depths of my belly.

"I have a place—well, for a little while, anyway."

"Great," I grunted. "Where?"

"The bartender's girlfriend. She lives out on the Avenues."

Saying nothing, I shut my eyes.

"You don't look too good," Marie said.

"I'm not," I told her.

"Do you want anything?" she asked, turning towards the kitchen.

"Yeah," I whispered.

"What?"

"Don't go."

She looked at me for a few seconds, not once changing expression, and walked off.

I watched her pack the few things she had into a flimsy green bag. I couldn't help but try and detain her in what otherwise would have been a clean break. "Marie, you don't have to leave right now," I told her.

"Better now than later, don't you think?"

I couldn't come up with a good enough reason so I sat there in silence.

"Well then," she said, walking towards me. I was waiting for her to deliver an ultimatum and hoping she wouldn't. I really wasn't sure what I wanted anymore.

"Here," I said, "I have something for you," and handed back the envelope with the photographs of the girl she had given me.

She took it and sat down on the couch. "How are you feeling?" she asked.

"A little groggy, why?"

"Do you really want me to stay?"

"Yes, I do."

"We'll talk about it tomorrow," she said, stuffing the envelope into her jacket pocket, "when I come back." And with that she turned, leaving her bag behind, and walked out the door.

The phone rang. I picked it up without opening my eyes. "No one is home right now," I announced. "If you wish to leave a message you may do so at the tone." I walked to the front door with the phone, opened it, reached around the frame and pushed the buzzer. "Marvin, I'm begging you. Please call," said the woman on the other end before she hung up.

Silence

When I got up the next morning Marie was already in the kitchen. I wondered where she had spent the night. I didn't even want to entertain the idea that she'd stayed with my ex-wife.

"I made coffee and bought some donuts," she said.

I surveyed the table and thought about why it was that every woman I had ever known found it necessary to state the obvious. Just then someone pounded on the door. Marie and I looked at each other for a moment before she got up to see who it might be. I heard the door open, then a commotion. The redhead ran by pushing Marie in front of her, yelling, "Hurry, hurry!"

They ran by again. "Go up to the roof," she ordered Marie who was clutching a small bag under her arm. Closing the door she turned to me and asked, "Where was Marie sitting?"

I pointed over to her place at the table. "What's going on?" She sat.

"I'll handle it," she said, before being interrupted by a knock at the door. She bolted up, pulled the "Have You Seen Me" poster from the refrigerator, crumpled it and threw it in the garbage, walking calmly to the front door to open it.

A man's voice. Then I heard her say, "No, detective, you don't have to do that, it's just that your visit's a little unusual. Please come in."

One of them sniffed around the apartment while the other followed her into the kitchen. "My husband," she said. After declining our offer of coffee and donuts the detective asked me what seemed to be "the usual questions," and when the other detective re-joined his colleague, reporting to him quite literally, "nothing," they both excused themselves, apologizing for any "trouble" they might have caused, and left.

The door shut and the phone began to ring. "I'm at the donut shop, I can see them getting into their car. I'll be over in a few minutes."

The phone rang again as soon as I hung up. "Marvin," the woman said, "I . . ."

I hung up again and walked into the kitchen.

"The coconut ones are best," the redhead said, picking a powdered donut from the box, then, "Hey beautiful," as Marie walked in, "do us a favor and grab that bottle from the cabinet on your way in."

"It's the money," Marie commented, taking a chair. "Since I'm a dependent my mother gets less money now with me gone. I'm sure that's it."

It didn't sound like a convincing argument but I let it go.

What followed was a conversation on the ins and outs of the system that I didn't really pay much attention to. When the redhead poured her second glass I knew where the afternoon was headed and excused myself.

Marie called out as I was opening the door to leave. "You're going out?" And then, before I could answer, she was at my side.

"Let me go with you?"

"And her?" I nodded towards the kitchen.

"She'll be all right," Marie said.

We walked over the hill towards North Beach with no particular destination. I was thinking about what those detectives would have done to me if they had found Marie. Maybe it would be better if she stayed somewhere else.

"You look worried," Marie said, reading my mind.

I shrugged my shoulders.

"I could go out to the Avenues if you're really worried," she said.

I shook my head. "I've got other things on my mind," I told her.

"Your translation?"

"That too."

"So tell me about Sayama." she said as we crested the hill.

"Next week," I said.

"Well, that doesn't seem like a reason to get anxious. You should be happy."

"Her husband's coming with her."

"I don't believe it," she said.

"She's going to leave him—stranded, you could say."

"I don't believe it," she repeated.

"Hey, that kind of stuff happens, and sometimes for the best," I replied, somewhat on the defensive.

"No, not only that," she said. "The bartender's girlfriend told me she met her second husband almost the same way. They got together after chatting on the Internet."

"You don't say," I said.

Then we walked the hills in silence. Marie put her arm around me and for once nothing else seemed to matter.

A Piece of Cold Steel

That night I worked on the translation and waited for Sayama to iron out the details. So far we'd decided I would meet her in Los Angeles and we'd drive back up to San Francisco in a rented car. She skidded across the screen with palpable excitement. For someone who had been railed through life like a freight train, this was a chance to disembark, for once, at the station of her own choosing.

"I count the days. I can hardly sleep anymore," she told me.

Later that morning, after my date with Sayama, the three of us sat at the kitchen table eating Dutch apple pancakes and breakfast sausage.

"Where did you learn to cook?" Marie asked the redhead, marveling at the spread laid out before us.

"Vacaville Correctional Facility," she answered, then asked me to pour her a drink.

When I got back to the kitchen with the bottle they were talking about reincarnation. "I think I was the worm at the bottom of the mescal bottle," the redhead said.

"I don't know if I like the idea." Marie decided.

I tuned to the all-news station on the radio to get my bearings.

"Then you think there's nothing after you die?" she asked Marie.

The Dow Jones Index was down.

"I mean if there's something before and after life, why bother with being born?"

A passenger jet crashed into a runway in Santiago.

"You got a point there," the redhead said.

As they continued their conversation I got ready for a shift in Union Square. When I returned to say goodbye the redhead looked up and laughed.

"Hey, you sure got some kind of talent," she said.

"Thanks," I replied.

"No, I mean it. I've seen you in Union Square."

"Thanks," I said again.

"I was wondering what happened to you."

"And now you know."

She burst out laughing again and still hadn't finished when I closed the front door. I thought of Marie leaving and Sayama's arrival. To be honest, the idea of being with Sayama excited me still, but when I really tried to picture it, I didn't know that I wanted her to actually arrive. I played with the idea of suggesting she let me come to Japan first, before she made her decision. But I couldn't back off like that. We had already confirmed most of our plans and were down to the final details.

Then, it hit me like a hammer as the Square came into view. On the wall opposite my spot was a silver man. Even his costume was similar to mine. I quickened my pace, ready to physically remove him from his perch. I walked up and we stood face to face. "Get the fuck out of here!" I stated. He didn't blink. "You heard what I said?" I screamed into his ear. He didn't move, not even a muscle. "Fuck you and the syphilitic whore who had you, you fucking thief." He still didn't even flinch.

He was good, no doubt about it. A crowd had gathered and a few people even threw coins into his hat. I wanted to kick it over but that would have been going too far, even for me, so I did the next best thing. I took my position up on the wall opposite him. Standing on one leg I stretched my arms out and leaned forward. As I stared over towards the corner of Powell and Geary I could hear people all around me exclaim, "Look at that!" Then I heard the coins, at a fairly steady clip, drop into my hat. After several minutes my leg started to ache but I kept it up, just to show the competition that, for me, there was no competition. The satisfaction I got from knowing he could hear the coins dropping over on my side while people passed him by enhanced my endurance. After awhile I began to hear an almost equal number of deposits into his hat. When I couldn't stand it any longer I brought down my leg and turned to look at him. He was standing on his head.

I should have gone and pushed him over. Instead I picked up my hat, walked across the street to where the panhandler sat with his, "Have AIDS. Doing The Best I Can. Please Help" sign, gave him the money I had earned and started for home.

I didn't think it possible to feel even more displaced then I already felt, but I did. About a block before my building I noticed the same two detectives from the day before, sitting in an unmarked car. I walked right by and it didn't seem like they noticed me under the gold makeup. When I got inside I told Marie and the redhead we were being staked out.

"Yeah, we saw them circle the block a few times," the redhead said. "Don't worry, we're keeping an eye out."

Marie frowned, obviously feeling some sort of noose tightening around all of us.

I left both of them in the kitchen while I went to take a shower. Marie got ready for her job at the FotoStop. I wondered if she knew more about the appearance of the detectives than she let on. It seemed to me that they were putting more time into this particular case than it warranted. I was undecided about whether to ask her or just let it go.

Leaving the redhead to nurse her bottle in the company of the television, I polished off what remained of the translation. Later, I walked down Polk Street and waited for Marie.

"How was work?"

"Okay."

"I left your friend back at the apartment. She's doing her best to drink all my booze."

"Yeah, she seems pretty much set on drinking herself to death."

"She's not alone," I said.

"You know, I think sometimes it's just a reaction."

"What? Her drinking?" I queried, suspicious.

"Yeah," she answered, "I think you make her nervous."

"She hides it well."

"Well, it's not exactly that she's afraid of you, it has more to do with me and you."

"How do you mean?" I asked.

"She's afraid of getting hurt. She's in love with me."

"I'm not surprised."

We walked on in silence for a while. Marie grabbed my hand. "Would you mind accompanying me?" she asked almost formally.

"Accompany you where?"

We continued without a word to a bus stop and waited. I watched her at the curb looking for the bus while I sat on the bench smoking a cigarette. She had changed in the short time that I'd known her. All she needed now was someone to give her a chance and she would be alright.

"Here it comes," she said.

She knew where she was going, that much was clear. We were in a part of the city—a hilly residential area of one-family homes off Upper Market, with winding streets, dead ends and cul-de-sacs--that I was thoroughly unfamiliar with. At the second to last house on a street that ended in steps to a higher one above it, Marie stopped. "This is it," she said.

"This is what?"

"The girl's address—from the photos."

"What are we going to do?" I asked, a little nervous.

"The girl's name is Emily," she said, not answering my question

She sat down on the curb across from the house and I sat next to her.

"What time is it?" she asked.

"Almost eleven-thirty."

"Good."

I was worried. Besides whatever Marie had planned, it was the kind of neighborhood where the neighbors were likely to call the police. It was also the kind of neighborhood, judging from the large two-story homes, where the police actually responded to those types of calls.

"Okay," she said suddenly, "follow me."

We moved up the street a little ways, to some steps that led up to one of the houses on the other side of the street. Two overgrown shrubs flanked either side of the walkway, keeping us hidden from view.

"What are we doing?"

"You just watch," she said.

The porch light came on at the house we were keeping an eye on. When the door opened I saw a man with a dog on a leash step outside. He descended to the street holding back the terrier by its leash as it strained towards the hill.

"Are you watching?" she whispered.

I shook my head.

We sat stock-still as the man and the dog passed without noticing us. A slight but well-built man of medium height, with short brown hair and glasses. I recognized him from the photos. There had been one with him holding a kite, another with one arm around the girl, Emily, and his other arm around a woman who let you know what Emily would look like in another twenty-five years.

Marie watched him with an intensity I thought he must be able to feel on his back. I reached out to take her hand and calm her but instead of warm flesh my hand grabbed a piece of cold steel. I looked over at Marie.

"Let's go," she said, without any worry of being discovered, then stood and pulled me up. When we got to the end of the street, right before turning the corner, she reeled around and brought the gun up, eye level, with two hands, taking aim at the man who was coming back down the street. I watched in horror. We were too far away for the man to make out the gun. I wanted to run. I wanted to wrestle the gun away from Marie.

"Pow," she said, then spun around and began walking back to the main street we had come from.

Waiting for the bus, I wondered if the gun had anything to do with the detectives who had been hanging around. If she had shot the man from where we stood he wouldn't have known what hit him. Maybe it had been the same for my brother. Before he even realized everything was over. It was that simple and still it was hard to believe. After we boarded the bus, Marie looked out the window as if nothing had occurred.

"I thought you were going to shoot."

"So did I."

Something to Turn Back to

I ambled into the living room and poured myself a drink. The redhead turned over in her sleep grumbling. I took a seat at the edge of the coffee table and turned on the TV to take my mind off of things.

An earthquake in Iran. Men in suits in Washington. Farmers dumping potatoes on a highway. A student riot in Korea. Men in suits in Brussels. I watched without the sound until Marie strolled in and the redhead all of a sudden sat bolt upright on the couch and screamed, "Gimme that!" Then sat there, rigid, with her eyes wide open.

She wasn't conscious. Marie walked over and shook her by the shoulders, yelling, "Hey, wake up! Snap out of it!"

And she did. She literally shook herself awake. The spent tension of her body collapsed into its normal state; she looked up at us, bleary-eyed, and asked for a drink. Marie heated a can of soup and made coffee.

“Turn up the sound, would you?” the redhead asked.

We watched an old Hayley Mills picture, the one that gave them the idea for The Patty Duke Show. Hayley plays twins. Marie curled up and laid her head on my lap. The redhead stretched out and put her feet on the table. Separated twins meet accidentally and scheme to bring their parents back together. It made me think about us on the couch watching them. What would Hayley Mills do?

Both of them drifted off a little before sunrise. I poured a drink and went into the kitchen to stock the Mr. Coffee coffee machine with some strong brew. It was almost time to talk to Sayama.

There was a palpable weight to the silence. Outside, it seemed the fog would never burn off; instead the peninsula would become wrapped in it, cut off from the rest of the world. The street noise was muffled and bounced back in warm tones at odds with the weather. This was the kind of day I liked best, when the true character of the city shows itself, gently pushing people indoors, piling them up in cinemas and cafés and wreaking havoc on tourists' vacations.

We arranged to meet on a Santa Monica street corner that I got from an ad in a phone book at the library. Since her husband had plans for a day of golf with friends of friends, Sayama decided she'd leave a note saying she had gone shopping, and if all went according to our predetermined strategy, we would be long gone before he would even suspect anything.

It was hard to imagine those first few moments that would start our new life: opening the car door, getting in, taking off on a freeway heading north.

"This is becoming difficult," she told me, "saying goodbye in my head without telling people I might not ever see them again."

I swallowed hard. "Are you sure, do you have many doubts?"

"I have to tell myself the decision is the right one," she replied. "What I do know is the decisions I made to get me where I am today were not so good."

I didn't have the courage to tell Sayama what I really wanted. Thinking back, I don't think I was clear with myself, what I did or didn't want. The earnest tone of our scheming left little room for the tender relationship that we'd always had, and I felt more than a little askew after our conversations about logistics.

I couldn't help feeling similarly to how I felt after my brother's death. It was only then that I realized that with a few simple words I could have forgiven him. Not that it would have helped him any, or changed what happened, but it might have cleared a way for learning how to accept things on their own terms, something that eluded me then and even now.

After turning off the computer I looked up on my wall at the line of frames containing my butterfly collection. Dozens of beautiful deaths caught in an eternal transformation of color and flight. I remembered my brother making fun of my interests. His attraction was to fast cars and power—truth was I only discovered a tender side to his character after his death. And it was only during his wake that I remembered him teaching me how to ride a bike and shag fly balls. I hoped Sayama and I could hold on to some of what we had.

I prepared myself to go down to Union Square, leaving Marie and the redhead sprawled across the couch. It was still early and I decided to take some air before getting to work. The fog clung to the hillsides and the tops of the buildings in the valleys were shrouded in mist. The top of Russian Hill reminded me of the Golden Horn. Unseen ships hauling unknown cargoes announced their presence with bellowing calls—music mysteriously unleashed from the restraints of song. Not even the brashest billboard or the most innocuous musical loops blasting Beach Boy tunes from the doors of novelty shops for tourists could dispel the mood.

"Hey Father, long time no see," the bartender called out from the doorway.

"You're here early," I said.

"I open today and I have to clean up first."

I nodded.

"Did you hear? I'm getting married."

"Congratulations," I told him.

"How's Marie?"

"Doing the best she can."

"She stayed with us the other night. Seems like my girl and her have a lot in common."

"I bet they do," I replied.

"They sat around jawing for hours."

"About what?"

"You know," he said, obviously embarrassed. "I didn't pay much attention."

I raised an eyebrow and tightened my lips. "I've got to be going."

"I've seen you at Union Square," he called after me. "You're really good."

The panhandler nodded just before I crossed over Powell, and I pulled a dollar from my pocket.

I could feel the fog burning off as I sat there with my head in my hands. The invisible city that I felt so at home in slowly disappeared, replaced by a profusion of sight and sound as the familiar world of common occurrence re-emerged.

The bright faces of visitors, free from the monotony of well-lit offices in neat little towns, passed by smiling, with purchases from nationally known retailers, their children trailing behind them clutching balloons and pretzels and hot dogs. Sometimes they almost seemed to be miming the mime that worked the Square as they wandered among the tediously sketched drawings of disintegrating vessels rocking on small swells at anchor in the bay. All this commerce and need had a certain charm under the bright sun for those who were only passing through.

I barely paid attention as I was caught in the click of the camera's shutter. But sometimes I wondered how many homes I now inhabited across the country. Did I permeate their lives, or they mine? Did they relate to the stiff competition for a quarter? For the quarter of a percent of the cash they had just shelled out to Tommy Hilfiger? They would go back home and smile upon seeing me, more than I could say of my best wishes for them.

"Hey," someone called out. The sound penetrated my cloak of concentration by the sheer persistence of repetition. "Take a break." I looked down. It was Marie.

"I've been standing here for half an hour and you didn't even notice me."

"What are you doing here?"

"I came to see you."

I hopped off the wall, happy to see her. "How did you like the act?"

"It's something else," she said.

"Are you hungry?"

She gave a hint of a smile and we walked over to a place on Kearny at the edge of Chinatown where I knew the owner. I wanted to ask her about the other night and the gun, but didn't. She told me someone had called and left the message, "It's your move." I convinced her to eat the long beans she pushed around her plate and eventually finished after the first few timid bites.

"Let's go for a walk," I suggested.

"Sure," she said.

We wound through North Beach and skirted the Wharf as we made our way towards the park. We sat down on the break wall along the narrow beach. Joggers with water-resistant fluorescent jackets and iPods, their dogs trailing behind them, ran by one after the other.

"I need to decide what to do with my life," she began. "And what will you do when Sayama gets here?"

"I don't think I want her to come," I confessed. "I was interested in something else, but now that's gone. Her being here is going to erase everything we had."

"Do you ever think about me and you?"

"Yeah," I replied

"What?"

"Things that can never come true."

"I already miss you," she said. "I want to convince you, beg you even… but…"

I put my arms around her. We watched an old man in a wetsuit dive into the water and swim, with steady, rhythmic strokes, out to the buoy.

"Why can't we just stay like this forever?" she whispered.

I took her by the hand and we walked, arm in arm, home. Not a word passed between us after we left the bay. In the lingering silence of my bedroom I undressed her. We made love, slow and deep and sad, with the half-light barely filtering through the sheers on my windows. She was crying and I kissed her tears away, both of us, it seemed, afraid to break the quiet. We were marking the moment, imprinting it on our senses, something to turn back to, privately, in the future, when we began to lose sight.

While He Slept

He was an odd man, Marie thought as he lay beside her. It was early evening and everyone was asleep. The only sound in the apartment was the redhead snoring from the living room, drunkenly buried in her latest stupor.

She called work and asked for the day off. It was the first time in a long while she felt at peace with herself. She needed time to work things out. She assumed the visit from the detectives was Mariel or Mary's doing, since they were the only ones who knew where she was. In effect, it closed the door on an era and place she felt increasingly alienated from. She would never go back. As for Steve… well, she just didn't know. Her only misgiving was her younger sister. For her alone she thought, she would have no trouble pulling the trigger, if it came to it.

In some ways she blamed her father. When he left, Marie's mother insisted she stay in school while complaining about having to humiliate herself by taking welfare and cleaning houses. She would remind Marie that as a girl in Nicaragua, she'd had a live-in maid. "Now look at me."

With Steve the golden words were, "He makes good money." That's what had sealed their fate, a steady paycheck. They all seemed weak to her now—without the strength to face hard truths. The importance of family and responsibility that she had been so harshly schooled in was reduced to empty words.

Looking over at him sound asleep she couldn't help but smile. If she had one wish it would be to be fifteen years older. More than anything she wanted to stay but she knew she had to move on, for her own good. Still, she marveled at their circumstances. How they had found each other by sheer luck. And how, despite his introversion and penchant for disguise he was brutally honest and straightforward. The fact was that she had never felt loved until now.

The whole experience had let her see the muddled circumstance of her life differently. His determination to go on regardless of the past was nothing less than inspirational, to her if not to himself. As for her redheaded friend in the other room, she was already gone. Marie could only lend her a small degree of comfort. With the other kids at work, so different from her, she felt resentment for their strength and buoyancy, qualities that had been robbed from her before she even knew they existed. And yet, despite their worldliness, Marie felt herself a citizen of the unsteady firmament of life they had yet to discover. And then there was Emily…

Emily was like a shadow of herself, both the same and the reverse. To look at those photos made her want to cry. She knew the dark, silent spaces that ate away from the inside. The secrets that people think can't be told, and the powerlessness of being trapped somewhere so awful that denial is the only way to get through it.

Now, though, she had the power to decide for herself and Emily didn't.

He rolled over onto his stomach and mumbled something. It sounded like a complaint but she couldn't tell. The one thing she knew was that there was nowhere in the world she would rather be.

Like a Virgin Bride

It was early morning and I watched as her gold-tinged body stretched across my bed. When she stirred, and finally opened her eyes, I said, "Let's leave. Get out of town."

"Where do you want to go?"

"I don't know, take the train to the end of the line."

"Hayward," she said.

"Ever been there?"

"No," Marie answered.

"Let's go then."

When we were in the station looking at the regional transit map, we opted for Concord instead. It resounded of grapes and revolutionary fervor. Marie bought a Snickers bar and some Peanut M&M's for the ride. Someone had left a paper on the seat and we sat down and read the *Oakland Tribune* while shooting through a tube at the bottom of the bay. It felt like we were headed for another country.

When we surfaced on the other side there were rows and rows of houses. Within three-quarters of an hour we reached our destination. Crossroads with specially timed lights that gave a mysterious order to the flow of traffic. Shopping malls with underground garages. We wandered into a food emporium and sat in their "café."

"Concord," Marie said.

We wandered past racks of clothes, shelves of electronics, bins of compacts, cans of food, displays of sporting goods, popcorn stands, photo booths, restrooms, Pizza Hut, Radio Shack, a chalet and a castle, and out the door into the heat of the carbon-monoxide haze, back to the train.

Berkeley was better. We found a big patch of grass under some trees at the edge of the university campus. I'd bought a six-pack on the way up.

"And what will you do if it doesn't work out with Sayama?" she asked, watching an ant run the length of her index finger.

"I don't know. I hadn't thought of it."

"Well you should," she said, putting her fingertips together, watching the ant's determined march to nowhere, "your track record isn't that great."

"And what have you decided?" I asked.

She shrugged. "I guess I'd like to find somewhere where I feel okay, get a job, go to school," she took a sip from her beer, "You know, nothing special."

We finished the six-pack and walked down the grassy knoll, sluggish and sleepy, to the avenue. It was a warm night and the streets were crowded with handicraft vendors, panhandlers, kids with guitars and skateboards and petitions. A lady blew bubbles and recited poetry outside a used record store.

"Let's not go back to San Francisco," I suggested. We only had a few more nights together, although I didn't mention it. "We can stay in a hotel."

"Okay." Marie smiled.

Our transition out of the ordinary was instantly made real by the fact that we happened to be standing in front of a hotel. I walked up to the counter, put my credit card on the desk and asked for the honeymoon suite.

"Will the Evergreen suite be suitable?" the clerk asked.

"With a bottle of champagne."

"Your bags?" He signaled the bellhop over.

"The chauffeur will bring them later," I replied.

"Of course," the clerk said and nodded. "Have a pleasant stay."

Our room overlooked the spectacle of Telegraph Avenue. When the champagne came I asked room service to bring us a pizza from across the street. Marie and I left the champagne on ice and took a shower. We wrapped ourselves in thick bath towels and left the French doors open.

When the pizza came we rolled the little cart over to the bed and opened the champagne. I dimmed the lights and made a toast. "To Marie," I said, holding up the glass.

"To us," Marie added.

It was something like an ending, at least that's how it felt to me as we took the train back to the city the next morning. Marie was irritable and didn't have much to say. When we got back home the redhead lifted her head off the couch and asked, "Who the fuck is Marvin?"

Marie walked off into the bedroom and I went into the kitchen to make coffee.

"Where were you guys?" the redhead asked the air. No one answered. Her presence had begun to grate on me—not that it hadn't before—but now I felt taken advantage of, thoroughly. I thought back to our one night together and was disgusted with myself. Had she told Marie about it?

I cleared the mess from the kitchen table and when I opened the garbage, found two liquor bottles that had been full the day before. I walked into the living room, collapsed onto the sofa and poured myself a drink from a half-empty vodka bottle.

"Did you guys at least have fun?" she asked.

"Did you?"

She looked at me, hard, a wounded look on her face. It occurred to me that this might be how Marie would end up.

"If you want me to leave all you have to do is say so."

The vodka was sharp on my tongue and burned deep inside of me after I swallowed.

"Well do you?" she asked.

I couldn't answer. It was true I didn't want her there but it was also obvious she had no one, and besides where would she go? I didn't even know where she had come from.

"Okay, I'm gone," she said, picking up her bag and ambulating unsteadily towards the door.

"Where are you going?" I asked.

"Home. Where else?"

"And where's that?"

"The Hartford, on Polk and Larkin."

I walked to the door with her. "Listen, I'm really sorry. I just want to be alone for a little."

"Don't sweat it."

After the door slammed I went to check on Marie. She was curled up on the bed facing the wall. I walked back into the living room to collect myself and finish my drink. I wondered when it would stop. I really had no other option than to wait and do what I could in the meanwhile.

I grabbed the remote and clicked on the television. The phone rang.

"You never called me back," my mother started in.

"I've been busy."

"With drinking?"

"No, with work."

"So you found a job."

"You could say that."

"Well either you did or you didn't."

"I'm working on some translation from my home."

"Don't you think it's time you had a real job?"

"And what do you mean by a real job?"

"You know, one where you get up in the morning and go to work."

"That's what I do, only I don't leave the apartment."

Talking to my mother almost always made me want to get drunk. After hanging up I thought I might sample some of Marie's marijuana. I rolled a joint and sat down to smoke it while watching *Leave It to Beaver*. It was very strong and with each inhalation I coughed out smoke. After I finished it, I could hardly keep my eyes open. I lay my head back on the pillow and stretched out on the sofa.

When I awoke, I sleepwalked into the bedroom and crawled into an empty bed. Marie was gone and my head was pounding. The phone was ringing but I didn't bother. I don't know how long I slept but when I got up I felt exhausted. I put on some coffee and took a cold shower, and realized I had lost track of the days and missed Sayama two days in a row. Then I thought, what if I discontinued contact with her altogether? Looking up at the kitchen clock, I saw it was just about time and settled in dutifully at my computer after pouring a cup of coffee.

"Where have you been?" she asked. "I was worried about you."

"Just some things that needed taking care of."

She didn't press for specifics.

"I missed you," she said.

"Are you almost ready?"

"Ready as I'll ever be."

"It sounds like you're nervous."

"Aren't you?"

"Like a virgin bride," I said.

The Ponderous Heft of the Dream

Things were coming to an end, or a beginning. The phone rang and when I picked it up she began, "Marvin," like always.

"Get off my back!" I screamed, "Don't you get it?" then I took the receiver and banged it, repeatedly, against the wall yelling, "Leave—me—alone!"

Marie came into the room and took a seat on the other side of the sofa. It was already late afternoon. We looked at each other and it was as if we had nothing to say, or maybe we were afraid to say it. There were only a couple of days left—so what was the use? I felt like I had on the plane flying away from my ex-girlfriend and my brother. Heightened anticipation mixed with a gripping fear.

I retrieved the phone and dialed. "Yeah," he answered.

"I'm forfeiting the game."

"What?"

Before I could get another word out of my mouth he had already hung up.

"So when do you need me to clear out?" Marie asked, as if we were discussing the most mundane of household chores.

"I'll be renting a car and driving down in a couple of days," I answered.

"So what do you think?"

"What do you mean?"

"This is it, what you've been waiting for."

"I don't know."

"Now ain't the time to get cold feet."

I looked up and smiled. "It's just that I didn't expect what happened to happen."

"You'll be okay," she said. "It's probably what you need the most right now."

I looked at her hard for a second, to remember. I couldn't help but think I was pulling the rug right out from under her. There was no easy way out for us, it seemed there wasn't any way out at all except a cold, clean break—like none of it had ever happened.

"And you?" I asked, timidly.

She shrugged. "I'm still thinking. There are plenty of options."

"Think you'll go out to the Avenues?"

"Yeah, for a little while," she volunteered nonchalantly. "Why are we talking about all of this anyway?" she asked, slightly annoyed. "We still have two days. Take a shower, and let's get out of here."

We walked down to Market, found a café, and sat at a back booth while Marie rattled on at an accelerated clip, skirting the edges of her life. Her chatter was as amusing as it was disconcerting. It was her strong card. An honest and artful dodge by turns disarming and aggressive. As she went on I was reminded of the things I would miss the most.

"My cousin claims that his father changed his name and went to live in Texas."

"The one that jumped off the bridge?"

"He played detective and actually went all the way down there and found a lady with two children, whose husband had been murdered gangland style for no apparent reason. She hardly knew anything about his life, family or friends, before she met him."

"Interesting, but doesn't sound convincing enough," I said spearing a slice of bacon.

"Same shoe size, he matched the ten-year-old photo with the ones she showed him, he was convinced."

"And your aunt?"

"She wasn't, though she admitted, looking over photos, that it was possible."

"She wouldn't know what her own husband looked like?"

"She had become a different woman by then."

"What do you mean, 'a different woman'?"

"She joined a church where they speak in tongues."

"Oh," I said.

After we finished eating we drifted through Hayes Valley to window shop, stopping to read menus posted outside restaurants and look into bars, winding past the Opera House and City Hall, towards South of Market. She talked about getting back into school. Next year she would be eighteen and no one could touch her. She rattled off a list of jobs she could possibly do until then, leaving little room for all the things I wanted to ask. She deftly sidestepped openings in the conversation, softly shutting doors before any air could come in.

We skirted the edges of the green oval at South Park. A woman with a fake fur and a man in a leather bomber jacket sat at an outdoor table over glasses of wine and argued. Down the block, two men wearing respirators in front of an opened roll-up door sprayed the side of a delivery truck. We crossed under the bridge, the lower span humming thirty feet above our heads, and continued in the direction of China Basin. The whole zone was in flux, rave spaces and leather clubs were being taken over by architects and lawyers who ripped down the old hand-painted signs in favor of gold lettering and the word "associates." A bulldozer stood in the middle of a gated plot where a community garden had once flourished. I pointed out all the old open spaces, now fenced in along the bay. Sometimes in the early evenings before "development" I would admire the brightly colored plastic pails surrounding the old Chinese men who fished the waters.

Skirting the edge of the bay, we ducked into one of the bars– the last one in fact that had managed to escape the city's blue-penciled plans for demolition and redevelopment. Dockside, I ordered burgers and beers and no one bothered to check Marie for ID. A stiff wind bounced small craft along the wharf that led up to the bar. Across from us, a rusting tanker rested in dry dock while some workers perched on a hanging scaffold and welded rivets.

"I used to come here with my father," Marie said, looking out at the water. "He would drink beer with a few friends and give me bread to feed the seagulls."

It seemed she wanted to say something more but stopped herself. Leaning into the wind, her hair gone wild, she pursed her lips and squinted out towards the sparks raining off the blowtorches by the iron sides of the ailing ship. All of a sudden, I was taken with her physical beauty. Dark, thick-lipped with oval eyes. Then she turned and regarded me with a tight, quizzical smile. Her gaze dug deep; somehow it was different from the other times. There was a hint of longing, bitter-edged and defiant, a complexity revealing where the last stronghold of innocence had been ransacked. I took her hand in mine and kissed it, and she looked away from me, towards the bay. The fading sky sank endlessly into the brackish water.

It was dark, with the thinnest sliver of a moon rising into drifting clouds before being erased. As we headed up Brannan, I could barely make out the yellow glow from the third floor of a factory building, like an apparition down the desolate street, two blocks away. As we got closer we saw people in the windows and heard jungle rhythms with spectral forms moving under a "Come To Where The Flavor Is" billboard, up on the roof.

I pushed the double metal doors apart and shrugged my shoulders when Marie asked where we were going. We moved past groups of people crouched on the concrete stairwell to talk or smoke, and entered the main room. The red brick walls seemed as if they were built from shadows under the black lights. The only fixtures, so to speak, were the DJ's suspension system with two turntables, and the six concrete supports that ran the length of the room. About three hundred people danced furiously, like they could somehow hold on to it with the animus of their movement, before it all disappeared.

Marie let herself loose on the dance floor and, after cavorting with her for a little, I tucked myself into a dark corner along the edges. The people around Marie were close to her in age, and I imagined I was witnessing a realm of possibility opening up for her. The casual contact, tantalizing suggestive gestures and signals of motion that surrounded her were sheer pleasure to observe.

The sun was already up by the time we hit the street again. Marie convinced me to stop at a diner before heading home. It was a night I knew from my own long-gone experiences—she didn't want to end. She ordered a stack of pancakes and ate quietly, as I sat sensing that same kind of lowdown sadness that we'd experienced after our trip to Berkeley.

If there was anything I was going to ask her, now was probably the time to do it. I let it alone.

We crawled into bed as the city came awake. As I drifted off I thought I heard the reversing turbines of a jet after it touched down on a runway. The next thing I remembered were trees rushing in a blur past my window. "You're going to crash," I cried. My brother looked over at me and said, "I know what I'm doing. Don't tell me." And suddenly it clicked. I tried to shout. I couldn't push the words out. Struggling, I tried to move towards him, pushing against the ponderous heft of the dream with all my might. Then, with my heart racing, I slowly came to consciousness, and there she was, looking down at me, one hand softly brushing back the hair stuck to my forehead.

"Are you okay?"

"It was my brother," I said, and she kissed me on the lips.

Gone

A world away Sayama was making last minute preparations. Or perhaps she was tossing next to her snoring husband before her life changed forever. We'd made plans to communicate one last time before she left.

I sat at the kitchen table, Marie across from me, flipping through a magazine while she sipped her coffee as if it were any other day. I didn't know what we should say or do but I thought things needed to be different.

"Any plans?" she asked without looking up.

"No," I answered, surprised by the question. "And you?"

"I have to go out for a while this afternoon. Will you be around tonight?"

"Yes." I was barely able to push the single syllable from my throat. "Would you like to do something special?"

"No," Marie said, "just hang out, watch television or… you know, something normal."

There were a thousand things to say but I couldn't bring myself to voice any of them. Instead, I wondered what it would be like once she was gone.

We cleared away the table and I switched on the radio to break the silence. Famine, genocide and an extramarital affair were at the top of the news. Marie left the room and I feared that Sayama would eventually become a repeat of my ex-wife. Life itself was not the mere resonance of emotion, and by turning this way and that, people fooled themselves into believing that the reshuffled order constituted reinvention. Maybe it was only our deciphering of the chaos that created order.

The phone rang and neither Marie nor I bothered to reach for it. My neighbor changed his mood that morning with a scratchy rendition of a klezmer orchestra. I laid down on the sofa and shut my eyes. When I was very young I believed that once I closed my eyes I became invisible—and part of me still believed it.

Marie, probably thinking I was asleep, quietly let herself out. Eventually, I got up, went into the bedroom and unzipped Marie's backpack. The gun was gone. Maybe that was a good thing. At the bottom of the bag, folded into a pair of jeans, were the photographs. I sat on the bed and stared at Emily, ignoring the constant ringing.

Later that afternoon I spoke with Sayama for the last time.

"Do you want to call me when you arrive?"

"No, just be there."

"Are you holding up okay?"

"I've never been so scared in my life. I don't know how I'm going to get through the next few days."

"Me either," I said, the typewritten message proving a poor conveyor of coloration and tone.

"And the girl?"

"She's gone," I lied.

The House of God

She heard the truck, an International straight job with a two-speed axle, before she saw it, double shifting with the weight of a full load. She stood up, took the gun out of her pocket, stepped towards the street and lifted it with two hands to take aim, making sure he got a good look at her. He veered, wildly, towards the opposite side of the street, sideswiping two parked cars while increasing his speed and trying to make the turn at the same time against the light. A dull metallic thud and a shower of glass followed the series of skids as Steve plowed into a passenger car in the middle of the intersection, and ended up on the sidewalk where he just missed hitting the corner building, diagonally across from her.

Before she could assess the results, she thought she had better get going. Slipping the gun back into her jacket, she backed away from the scene as calmly as she could manage.

No one came after her, and when she got to the bus stop two blocks away, she heard sirens.

She wanted to be alone. To work out what no one could help her with. She'd learned over the past few weeks that as far as the past receded it never entirely disappeared. Despite that, regrets could only be trumped by actions.

She changed buses at a downtown intersection and headed up the hill, toward somewhere she thought she could sit and mull over what needed to be done. Although she still couldn't put it together, she knew she was closing in.

She chose a bench on the far side of the park and looked out over Washington Square to the church across the neatly manicured lawn. She remembered that as a little girl, she used to pray.

In Marie's mind, even though the score didn't yet add up, everyone seemed to insist on a particular manner and order in which to proceed—suggested sets of parameters that needed to be adhered to. She felt like nothing was further from the truth. In fact, people who got what they wanted seemed to do precisely the opposite.

She couldn't help but think about Emily within this newly factored equation. She could already tell Emily would sacrifice herself to something she didn't really understand, no matter how terrible, to ensure at least some semblance of normality. When she thought of the girl she felt both sympathy and unrestrained rage.

She had thought of confronting the girl but realized nothing would come of it—or if it did, it might be for the worse. The construct—house, little dog, expensive clothes—the whole weight and shape of one's life seemed inextricably connected, but now, in her opinion it would be much easier to sweep away the debris than to step delicately around it. Choice, not fear, is the glue that holds things together.

With the sun casting long afternoon shadows, and the wind whipping kites with gusts that dashed them hard and sudden to the ground, she decided the only way to depend on the structure of things around you was to arrange it yourself. Then she got up, crossed the square, and walked into the church.

Where You're Going

"Maybe it would be better if I left now," she said, reading me wrong as I balanced myself on the edge of the couch unable to express what I felt.

"Sit down," I told her. The game was into the middle innings, one run down, two out and two men on. I put my arm around her, and gently pulled her head towards me so it rested on my shoulder. She shook a little under my weight, chest heaving, and although I tried not to look I spied the tears as they rolled off her cheeks. After that I could hardly control myself.

"I hate you," she cried, collapsing into my arms. "I hate you."

I kissed her on the neck, and breathed in the scent of her skin and hair. When we were finally able to look up, the Giants' half of the inning was over and they had failed to score.

After the game we ate a solemn dinner up the street at a corner luncheonette. Marie was pensive, shy even, and I didn't feel much like talking.

"Why can't we just live like other people?" she said, looking up from her plate.

"I think maybe we are," I answered.

"Maybe," she said.

As I watched Marie nibble away at her dinner, I thought about the depth of understanding I'd once believed was part of my relationship with Sayama. Now I realized it was nothing but the illusion of our hopes projected onto one another. I wondered if my brother and ex-girlfriend had ever had a realization like this one, considering the circumstances.

"You know, I really do hope it all works out for you," Marie said.

"Thanks."

"Really," she repeated. "And don't worry about me, I'll do what I have to."

"I know you will."

I wanted to continue and let her know how proud of her I was, and how I admired her, but swallowed my words with a swig of coffee that washed down the last of our final dinner.

Back home we watched CNN, more as a distraction than anything else. Marie got up and said she was going to bed. I would have followed, but I knew she wanted to transition the change in as mundane a manner as possible. This is it, I thought. I wished her a good night, and proceeded to watch the video feeds over and over, until morning.

A little after dawn I walked over to Taylor Street, picked up the car and parked as close to home as I could. Marie was already up, and just about to leave.

"I'll give you a ride," I said.

We fought traffic all the way out to Divisadero, and as we crested the hill on the Richmond side, we still hadn't said a word. A long grey band of fog settled out on the ocean, and before I turned the corner of my ex-wife's street, Marie said, "You can let me out here."

I pulled to the curb and she opened the door and jumped out. I leaned over and rolled down the window. "I'll call in a couple of days."

"Don't look so worried," she said, and I finally began to feel better.

Within twenty minutes I was on the highway heading south. I tried to shift my attention to Sayama but my mind kept drifting to Marie. I tuned the radio to a call-in show so I wouldn't have to think.

I tried to imagine Sayama's anxiety. They were probably in the middle of their breakfast, marveling at the selection of meat. Steak and eggs, I thought—the poor man. And then Marie. She was probably having coffee with my ex-wife at that very moment. I knew the feeling.

A caller on the radio said, "We should blow Baghdad to smithereens."

The continuance of things, I thought, heading south on the interstate, then its opposite.

It was a little before noon. A highway patrol flashed its lights behind me and I slowed down as he passed, throwing his steely glance my way. I pulled off at the next exit. I wanted a pause before it happened. Everything was set for four o'clock.

I got a coffee to go at a McDonald's and carried it to the car. As I was getting in, the highway patrolman pulled into the space next to me. He opened the door and stretched to his full height, never taking his eyes off me while I stood there.

"You'll never get to where you're going driving like that," he said.

"Sorry, I didn't even realize how fast I was going."

He nodded, and entered the McDonald's like a movie star dressed as a cop.

About Emily

The doorbell rang—chimed really—the moronic melody of the upper middle class. Marie leaned towards the door, listening for any sound that might be coming from inside. A car was in the driveway and she knew he was home. After dropping Emily off at school he would usually come back for about an hour to eat his breakfast, she imagined.

"Who is it?" she heard through the door.

"It's about Emily," she said.

"What?" he yelled.

"Emily," she shouted.

She heard the chain slide from the lock and the dead bolt turn. When he opened the door he seemed surprised to see a young girl on his doorstep.

"What about Emily?" he asked with concern.

"Mister," she said, "you hurt her real bad."

By the time he realized what was happening she had the gun leveled at his head. He fell backwards and somewhere she heard a dog bark. Without even registering the carnage she leaned forward, kicked one of his feet out of the way with the heel of her shoe, and pulled the door shut. Retracing her route down the sidewalk she slowly became aware of the blood splattered on her clothing, then brought her hand up to her face. It was sticky and wet.

Last Word

When I got back into the rental car and started the motor, I burst into tears. The last time I'd really cried was when I found out what my brother had done to me. I didn't know why but I felt like it was happening all over again. I was tired of running, escaping, telling myself everything was all right. Nothing was all right. I had let the person I cared for the most in the world leave only hours ago so I could chase a virtually perfect woman into a reality that probably didn't exist.

When the light changed, I drove past the southbound entrance ramp, under the overpass, and made a left turn at the sign for San Francisco. There was no way not to feel guilty, but I convinced myself that the worst that could happen to Sayama was she would realize she'd been stood up, and then she'd eventually find her way back to her husband. For her, I reasoned, the more lamentable fate would be to discover that the person behind the persona wasn't at all who she thought he was.

I considered calling Marie but decided just to show up. Explain what had happened, or not, and head home where we belonged. Everything would fall into place, I was sure of it.

Later that afternoon my ex-wife stood staring at me, as if I had woken her up from a bad dream. "What are you doing here?"

"Is Marie here?"

Hearing my voice, the bartender came to the door and stood by my ex-wife with a drink in his hand.

"Is she supposed to be?" she asked.

"Why don't you come in and have a drink with us?"

"You know him?" my ex asked the bartender.

As I was walking away I heard him explain, "Yeah, if it wasn't for him we'd have never met."

"What?" was the last word I could make out before getting into the car and driving off.

Saying It All Over Again

"Let's go over the whole thing just one more time, slowly," the man said, his hairy arms leaning on the table between them.

"Okay," she answered, tired of having to hear herself say it. She pointed at the photo in the middle of the table. "That's Emily," she began.

Marvin

"Marie!" I called out as soon as I got in. I shut the door behind me and poured myself a drink. Then I remembered the redhead, threw on my jacket and walked over to her hotel.

"She's in detox," one of her neighbors told me as I knocked at the door. "I saw them pick her up last night."

I dropped off the car and headed home to wait. I knew she had nowhere to go, and figured it was only a matter of time until she showed up. I spotted the schnauzer, crossing over Leavenworth at the top of Post. He came running down the hill and I stood there waiting for him. He stopped just short of me and I got down, hands on knees, and called, "Come on, boy."

He showed his two front teeth and started to growl. I patted my kneecaps with the palms of my hands. "C'mon." The pitch changed and he turned the volume up a notch.

I stood up and stamped my foot. He jumped back. I stood there, unflinching, and stared him down. He held his ground and gazed back at me. Maybe if he would come over, sniff around my feet, bury his wet nose into my hands... but he wouldn't budge. His body strained with the effort.

I picked up a rock, threw it, and missed. He took off back towards Post Street. I picked up another rock and missed again.

At home, I turned on the television to distract myself, and watched reruns of old sitcoms. After midnight, I began to drift off. It was probably past noon when I woke up for the first time. When I woke up again, I decided to go see the bartender.

"No, we haven't heard anything," he said, in a tone of voice that made it clear he didn't feel much like talking to me. I wondered what had passed between him and my ex.

I grabbed a bite to eat and headed home, trying to convince myself that she would show up, or at least call. I began to get edgy since it was all over with Sayama and, now that I had made my decision, Marie was nowhere to be found.

I poured a stiff one and settled in for the night.

It was an outside chance, but I didn't have any other options. Boarding the bus on California I thought of the night Marie had come to meet me after work. I wondered if she really had intended to shoot the man in the photo. I got off at the same stop and after wandering the winding streets for half an hour, finally hit upon the right one. I checked my watch. It was almost eleven, and I hurried up to where we had waited for the man to come out of the house.

The porch light came on and I heard the dog yapping. When they trotted by, I saw it was Emily this time with the dog. I wanted to say something but didn't know what.

By the next day I had the sinking feeling I might not ever see Marie again. At first it bothered me that she hadn't told me her plans, but as the day wore on I thought of it as a sign of strength. Something, one of the few decisions in her life, that was hers alone. My sadness, I realized, was for myself. I had lost what I most wanted, out of fear and my refusal to respond to my own emotions.

It was an empty feeling, being by myself on the couch. No work. No plans. I wondered what to do.

The nightly news with drinks—the usual—was the only course of action I could summon.

When the phone rang once I picked it up, expecting Marie.

"Marvin, I have to see you. I'm desperate," said the familiar voice on the other end. A silence, like a coda hung in the air. I knew how she felt. It had nothing to do with my brother's death, or Sayama, or Marie, but with something beyond our control.

I needed to put my arms around her, to forgive her, and be forgiven.

Our claim on the past was the only thing that might help propel us forward and away from abandonment's unrelenting hold. To trust her, despite what she had done, had something to do with shedding all my own disguises.

"You know the donut shop on Polk and Sacramento?" I asked.

"I do."

"Be there in ten minutes," I said, hung up the phone, and walked out the door.

©Alvaro Muñoz

About the Author

Albert Sgambati is a native of New York City. He divides his time between the US and Latin America, where he freelances as a film consultant, features writer, translator and editor. During the 1990's, he worked as a beat reporter for *The News*, in Mexico City. His writing has appeared in a range of magazines. His poetry has been included in *Anthology of American Poets 1980's*, Big Scream Press, Grand Rapids, and is featured in *All Roads…But This One*, a limited edition from Luddite Kingdom Press, San Francisco (2006). *The Waiting Room* is his first book.